Also by the Author

Aquarium

The Erin O'Reilly Mysteries
Book Twelve

Steven Henry

Clickworks Press • Baltimore, MD

First publication: Clickworks Press, 2021
Release: CP-EOR12-INT-H.IS-1.0

Sign up for updates, deals, and exclusive sneak peeks at clickworkspress.com/join.

Ebook ISBN: 978-1-943383-76-4
Paperback ISBN: 978-1-943383-77-1
Hardcover ISBN: 978-1-943383-78-8

This is a work of fiction. Names, characters, places, organizations, and events are either the products of the author's imagination or used in a fictitious manner. Any resemblance to actual persons, living or dead, is purely coincidental.

For Ron Cirksena, my 8th grade English teacher,
who always encouraged me.

Aquarium

Pour 2 oz. rum, 1 oz. Blue Curaçao liqueur, 1 oz. Lychee liqueur, and a dash of lemon juice into a cocktail shaker and shake. Strain into a cocktail glass and serve.

Chapter 1

"All right, you sorry lot of scunners. Shut your mouths and open your ears. I've something to say."

All eyes turned to James Corcoran, "Corky" to his friends. He stood on top of the bar at the Barley Corner pub, his curly red hair nearly brushing the ceiling, a glass of Glen D whiskey in his hand and a smile on his lips. Conversation quieted to a murmur, then died away into silence.

"As all of you know, our friend and proprietor, Cars Carlyle, has had some troubles of late. He's been a guest of New York's finest while recuperating from a very unfortunate injury. He's only just escaped from the hospital, and fortunately, the coppers didn't think it worth their while to pursue him. However, I do see they've a representative here among us today. But don't let that worry you, lads, she's one of us. You all know her. Stand up, Erin, love. Let the lads have a look at that stunner of a face."

Detective Erin O'Reilly stood and waved good-naturedly to the crowd of Irishmen. Her wave was answered by a loud cheer and a few appreciative wolf-whistles. But it was all in good fun. The faces she saw around her were friendly. Even if they hadn't been, she wouldn't have been worried. She was carrying two guns; one at her hip, the other in an ankle clip. And her partner sat right beside her, scanning the crowd for any sign of trouble. She might be at a party, but Rolf was on duty. He had keen eyes, great instincts, unbelievable reflexes, and the best nose in the NYPD. The German Shepherd was ninety pounds of well-trained law-enforcement muscle and teeth. He always had Erin's back.

"It's my understanding this lovely colleen saved my mate's life," Corky went on, drawing another cheer. "So it's only proper she's here for the lad's homecoming. Cars, lad, I don't know what you did to her that she fell for you instead of me. Think on it, lads. Look at my face, then look at his. I love him like a brother, but there's simply no comparison."

More laughter filled the room. On the other side of Erin from Rolf, Morton Carlyle just smiled and shook his head. In truth, he was at least as good-looking as Corky: a tall, silver-haired Irishman, impeccably dressed in a charcoal-gray suit and silk tie. He seemed perfectly healthy, his back straight as he sat on his customary bar stool. But Erin was close enough to see he still looked a little pale. A thin sheen of sweat stood out on his forehead.

She put out a hand and touched his arm. He met her eye and gave a very slight shake of his head, indicating she shouldn't say anything. It was important not to show weakness, not in front of these men. All of them were affiliated with Evan O'Malley's mob, most of them under Carlyle's own command.

"It's all right, lad," Corky was saying. "I forgive you for recovering and keeping me from comforting this poor, broken-hearted lass. And I want to welcome you, on behalf of all of us, back to your proper place. Had you died, I'd have drunk a toast hoping you'd made it to Heaven a full half-hour before the Devil heard you were dead. But you lucky bastard, you're still breathing. So instead, I'll make a different toast. May we all be alive at the same time next year."

Several dozen hands hoisted glasses. Erin raised her own, a glass of Carlyle's best top-shelf whiskey. It was a little early in the day for drinking, but when a cop had to fit in, what could she do?

"Oh, and here's me forgetting," Corky said, pausing with his glass halfway to his lips. "Poor Cars here was hurt in the liver, the very worst place for an Irishman. So we're in this fine public house, drinking his fine liquor, and he can't be partaking. Well, I'm a lad who knows his duty, so I'll take it upon myself to drink for him."

He immediately put his money where his mouth was, downing his own drink in a single gulp, then dropping nimbly off the bar, snatching Carlyle's glass up, and swallowing another shot. Carlyle patted Corky on the arm with an affectionate smile. The two men shook hands and bent in close for a one-armed hug, Corky taking care not to touch Carlyle's wounded abdomen. There was another enthusiastic cheer.

Carlyle slowly, carefully got to his feet. He raised a hand. Silence descended again.

"Thank you, lads, for coming to welcome me home," he said. "It's grand to be back. Drink up, have a grand time. And don't forget to tip your waitresses. It's a hard job they have, putting up with you sorry lot."

Amid another burst of laughter, he sat back down, wincing slightly. Erin took hold of his arm more firmly.

"You need to lie down," she said quietly.

"Aye, that's a fine plan," he whispered back. "Now that I've put in an appearance, we can be fading into the background. If you'd be so kind?"

Erin offered her arm. He took it, keeping up the pretense that he was assisting her instead of the other way around. Perception was everything in this world. Carlyle had to look strong. She had to look dependent on him. Both of them had to look like firm supporters of Evan O'Malley. Corky had helped with his "one of us" comment, which hadn't been an accident.

All of it was a lie. Carlyle had been released from Bellevue Hospital after eight days of recovery from the nasty gut shot he'd received in Erin's apartment. He was better than he had been, but nowhere near full strength. He was relying on Erin right now. And neither of them was on Evan O'Malley's side. Carlyle was a week into his new job, that of turncoat and informant. Corky was in on the secret, and though he wasn't happy about it, he'd supported them so far.

"Everybody's watching," Erin said in an undertone as they steered toward the door at the back of the room. Rolf trotted at Erin's side, ears perked, alert.

"Of course they are," he said, smiling pleasantly and shaking hands with several guys they passed. "It's just like being a politician, darling. Everyone's watching you, all the time. Some people enjoy that sort of thing."

"They're crazy," she said, keeping a bright, artificial smile plastered on her own face as she said it. "It's like living in a damn goldfish bowl."

"If you're a goldfish, that's a fine place to live," Carlyle replied.

"As long as there isn't a cat around," she said. "Did you see Mickey?"

"I noticed him, aye. Near the doorway, surrounded by his bully-boys. He didn't seem as pleased with my recovery as some of the lads."

Neither of them said why Mickey Connor was unhappy, but both of them were thinking it. They were convinced Mickey had orchestrated the attempt on their lives that had left Carlyle in the hospital. Mickey was Evan O'Malley's chief enforcer, a retired heavyweight boxer with a disturbing affinity for violence and a strong dislike of both of them.

"Are you all moved in?" Carlyle asked, unlocking his door and ushering Erin through.

"Yeah, I brought the last stuff over last night," she said. "I left some things in storage, and some others with my brother, but I'm out of my apartment. It's a little weird, staying here."

"Safest place you could be," he said. He took the stairs slowly and carefully. His abdominal muscles were still mending, which made climbing difficult.

"Doesn't feel that way," she said. "There's four dozen armed thugs out there right now, getting plastered. Doesn't matter that it's nine in the morning, they're getting drunk like it's midnight."

"Ah, but they're my armed thugs."

"They're Evan's," she corrected him.

"Not all of them."

"Enough of them. If they knew what we were doing…"

"But they don't."

Erin nodded, hoping he was right. If he was wrong, the first warning was likely to be someone taking a shot at one of them. But right now, she was just glad he was out of the hospital and on the mend. It was a sunny morning in May, the air was warm, and it was good to be alive.

She turned at the top of the stairs, looped her arms around him, and kissed him lightly on the lips. "It's grand to be home, isn't it?" she asked, deliberately using one of his favorite words.

"Aye," he said. "And give me a few days, I'll be back in fighting trim. For now, though, I fear I'm needing a bit of a lie-down."

"Sure," she said. "Anything I can get for you?"

He shook his head and started to say something, but was interrupted by her phone. Erin pulled it out and saw Lieutenant Webb's name on the screen.

"I better take this," she said. She'd arranged her schedule so she wasn't supposed to be at the precinct for another half hour. Something must have happened.

"O'Reilly," she said, swiping the screen.

"We've got a body," Webb said by way of greeting. "Downtown hotel. The InterContinental on East 48th, in Midtown."

"I'm on my way," she said. Hanging up, she gave Carlyle an apologetic smile.

"Go on, darling," he said. "I promise not to do anything exciting while you're away."

"I think we've had enough excitement for a while," she said. "Just be alive when I get back."

"You worry too much, darling. I'm the picture of health."

"I was thinking about the goons downstairs."

"And I told you, they're my lads. Take care of yourself."

"I'll be fine. It's the other guy you should worry about."

*   *   *

"This is definitely out of our price range," Erin told Rolf as they got out of her Charger and walked up to the front of the InterContinental Hotel in Midtown.

Rolf wagged his tail. He wasn't bothered by economic concerns.

"And they wouldn't let you stay here," she added. "You're too big. Good thing you're with me."

He kept wagging. Being with his partner was definitely a good thing. Maybe the best thing.

She hurried up the steps to the front door. She didn't see any sign of the police. Whatever had happened, it hadn't required a large uniformed presence.

In the lobby, she caught sight of a familiar trench coat and fedora. Under the hat, talking to a couple of hotel employees, was Harry Webb, Erin's commanding officer. Next to him loomed Vic Neshenko, the other detective on Erin's squad. Vic was watching the room and chewing a toothpick that was wedged in a corner of his mouth. He saw Erin as soon as she entered and nodded curtly to her.

Erin and Rolf joined the group. The hotel workers looked like a manager and a housekeeper. The maid was a young, pretty Latina. She was obviously upset. The manager had a hand on her shoulder in what Erin hoped was a fatherly, comforting gesture.

Erin offered her hand. "Detective O'Reilly," she said.

The manager took his hand off the woman and shook. "Nicholas Feldspar," he said. "Floor manager. This is Rosa Hernandez."

"Where did this happen?" Webb asked Rosa.

"The Ballroom," the young woman said. "The Grand Ballroom, that is. Not the Empire."

"You've got more than one ballroom," Vic deadpanned.

"On the mezzanine level," Feldspar put in. "We can go up those stairs." He pointed over his shoulder to an open staircase.

"Do I have to?" the woman asked. "It was so awful."

"I'm afraid so, Rosa," the manager said gently. "These people need our help."

"It'll be helpful if you can tell us exactly what you saw," Webb said.

"Nobody's in the room now, are they?" Vic asked.

"One of your officers is up there," Feldspar said. "He's keeping everyone else out."

"Good," Webb said. "Let's go."

"Glad you could join us," Vic said to Erin as they followed Feldspar to the stairs.

"How long have you guys been here?" she asked.

"Just got here," he said. "We don't know much. Apparently our girl was doing some cleaning in the public spaces. Y'know, since it isn't checkout time yet, she can't do the rooms. Anyway, she found a floater."

"A floater?" Erin echoed, not sure she'd heard him right.

He shrugged. "That's what I heard."

"Vic, we're not on the waterfront. In the swimming pool maybe?"

"Maybe. But she said ballroom." He shrugged again. "I guess it beats back alley murders. Ugly thugs are always getting popped. It's nice to hang around the beautiful people for a change."

They got to the top of the stairs. The manager led the way to the ballroom. Sure enough, a uniformed cop was standing outside the entrance, hands clasped at his belt buckle. Webb showed his gold shield and the uniform got out of the way.

The ballroom was as large and fancy as Erin expected, well-furnished and expensive. It was just on the right side of too much, coming across as tasteful rather than extravagant. The south wall was what drew her attention. The hotel had replaced that whole wall with glass, behind which was a massive aquarium, lit from beneath with a soft blue glow. Tropical fish drifted in place or darted around in flashes of bright, dramatic color. In the middle of the aquarium, arms outstretched, hair floating out in all directions, a woman hung suspended in the water. A diaphanous dress billowed around her. In the blue light her skin looked pale and unearthly, like a porcelain doll. She might have been asleep, but her eyes were open and staring right at the detectives.

"Jesus," Vic muttered. "That's creepy."

"You said you wanted to hang out with the beautiful people," Erin said very quietly.

"Not what I meant," he said.

Chapter 2

"This has never happened before," Feldspar said.

"You've never had a guest die?" Vic asked, raising a skeptical eyebrow.

"Well, yes, of course. I mean, we have the occasional heart attack. And there was that one woman, in the bathtub... very unfortunate."

"Bathtub?" Webb prompted.

"Her wrists," Feldspar said. "The cleaning staff found her, just like this one. It was terrible, but this... She might have chosen a more discreet way to end things."

"You're assuming this is a suicide?" Erin asked.

Feldspar flinched at the blunt word. "Of course. I mean, what else could it be?"

The three detectives looked at him in silence.

Feldspar laughed nervously. "Well, I mean, of course she did this to herself."

"You got a degree in forensic medicine?" Vic asked. "Taking night courses to become a doc?"

"Well, that is to say... no. No, I don't. I'm not."

"Did you see her jump in the tank?"

"I... no. Of course not."

"Then this is just a suggestion," Vic went on. "But how about you let the professionals decide what happened?"

"Do you know who this woman is?" Webb asked.

"I'm afraid not," Feldspar said. "Though I don't know all our guests by sight, of course."

"How did she get in the tank?" Erin asked. She walked up to the glass and peered into the aquarium. It extended all the way from floor to ceiling with no door or access hatch on this side.

"I don't know," Feldspar said. "I can put you in touch with Maintenance. They'll know how to access the aquarium."

"May I go now?" Rosa asked quietly. She was standing close to the doorway, turned so she didn't have to look at the ghostly floating body.

"When, exactly, did you find her?" Webb asked.

"A few minutes after eight," she said.

"Was anyone else in this room when you came in?"

"No."

"And she was just like she is now?"

"Yes." Rosa shuddered. "Please, may I go?"

"In a moment. You didn't recognize her?"

"No."

Webb's face softened. "Okay. You can go. Thanks for your help."

The housekeeper gratefully hurried out of the room. Vic joined Erin at the fish tank.

"It's not a swimming pool," he said.

"She's not dressed for a swim," Erin replied.

He nodded. "I don't see any injuries, but the water would've washed the blood out of them. She might have lacerations. There's so much water, it probably wouldn't be too pink even if she bled out. We better get Levine's take."

"Yeah," she said. "Weird way to kill yourself, if that's what happened."

"You wouldn't believe some of the creative ways people do it," Vic said. "I heard about this one guy, once, he shot himself in the chest without a gun."

"What'd he use? A crossbow?"

"Nope, a .22 bullet. Held it over his chest with a pair of pliers and whacked the bullet with a hammer."

"Did that work?"

"Sort of. The bullet went off and put a hole in him, but not in anything important. After a while, he figured he didn't really want to die so he walked himself into the emergency room."

"You shitting me?"

He shrugged. "I got it from an EMT who got it from the doctor who operated on him. They coulda made it up, I guess. Point is, if you want out bad enough, you'll find a way to do it. Why you think we take their shoelaces away when we stick 'em in lockup?"

"She's wearing a nice dress," Erin observed.

"Meaning what?" Vic asked. "She wanted to die? Or she didn't? You thinking she's like those hotel girls last year?"

"I don't wear dresses often," she said, suppressing a shudder at the memory. "And almost never that kind. Looks pretty fancy, doesn't it?" She turned to Feldspar. "Was there some sort of party here last night? In this ballroom, or maybe the other one?"

"Yes," he said. "There was a benefit dinner. A lot of wealthy donors to a charity."

"Which charity?" Webb asked.

Feldspar looked embarrassed. "I'm not actually sure. There are so many. I'll have to check the event roster."

"While you're doing that, if you could have someone from Maintenance come talk to us, that'd be helpful," Webb said.

"Of course, of course," Feldspar said. He got out of the room a little faster than was polite.

"You think he's our guy?" Vic asked.

"What? No!" Erin shot him a look. "What possible reason would he have?"

"I dunno. He looked shifty."

"He's nervous because there's a dead girl in his fish tank," she said. "You think he wants this sort of publicity for his hotel?"

"Hey, murder tourism is totally a thing," he said. "If the Bates Motel was a real place, they'd have reservations booked clean through next year. Am I wrong?"

"Not as wrong as you ought to be," Webb said. "But I don't think drumming up enthusiasm among murder aficionados is quite the motive we're looking for. We haven't even classified this as a homicide."

"She's dressed up," Erin persisted. "Either she was at a formal get-together or else..."

"...she was posed," Vic finished. "Yeah, I thought of that the moment I saw her. Spooky. But if it's posed, that means it's a serial."

"That's a stretch, Neshenko," Webb said sharply. Both Vic and Erin knew their Lieutenant's views on serial killers. He didn't like the media attention that kind of case brought, and he didn't like sensationalism.

"If it's posed, that makes it a homicide," Erin said. "We all agree on that?"

The other two nodded. Rolf, unconcerned, sniffed the floor and looked up at Erin. He thought they ought to be doing something that matched his definition of police work, which meant chasing and hopefully biting bad guys.

The uniformed officer poked his head into the room. "Uh, sir? Got a guy out here, says the manager sent him up."

"Let him in," Webb said.

"This isn't even the crime scene," Vic muttered. "We got

two inches of glass between us and the victim. If she was killed, it wasn't in here."

A stocky man with a two-day growth of stubble on his chin shambled in. He was wearing a blue work shirt and a pair of jeans, both well-worn. A nametag on his chest read NIMKOWITZ.

"Mr. Nimkowitz?" Webb guessed.

"That's me," he said. "What am I doin' here?"

"You work maintenance for the hotel?"

"That's right. Somethin' broken?" He scratched his chin.

"We need to know how to access this aquarium," Webb said.

"What for?" Nimkowitz's eyes drifted past Webb without much interest. Then he saw the floating woman and blinked. "Whoa."

"That's what for," Vic said. "Now, you gonna show us?"

"Sure," Nimokowitz said. "C'mon."

The maintenance man led them upstairs and along a hallway to a locked door, which he opened with a key from a ring in his pocket.

"Who else has keys to this room?" Webb asked.

"The custodial guys," Nimkowitz said. "Management, I guess. The electrician. All the support people."

"How many people are we talking about?"

Nimkowitz shrugged. "I dunno. Maybe eight or ten." He gestured. "In there, on the right. There's a trapdoor."

The room was dark. Erin found a light switch and flicked it on, bathing the area in harsh fluorescent light. It was obviously not a public part of the hotel. She saw lots of bare concrete and exposed pipes and valves. She also saw the trapdoor the maintenance guy had indicated.

"Closed," Vic said unnecessarily.

"Well, yeah," Nimkowitz said. "Those are tropical fish. The

tank's climate-controlled. See those dials there? That's temperature, pH balance, saltiness, you name it. We got a guy comes in from the Bronx Zoo to check on 'em once a week."

Webb knelt beside the trapdoor. He unlatched the door and pulled it open. The wet, fishy smell of a populated fish tank flowed into the room.

"No controls or handle on the inside," he said.

"Of course not," Nimkowitz said. "You don't want the fish escaping, do you?"

The detectives looked at him.

"That was a joke," he said.

No one laughed.

"What if someone falls in?" Webb asked.

"They could just swim out again," he said. "I mean, the door would still be open, right?"

There was a silence.

"Unless she got her hands on a key," Erin said, "and got into this room, and opened the trapdoor, and dropped through, and pulled it shut behind her..."

"Unlikely," Webb said. "This is looking like homicide. But we'll need the ME to sign off on it. Levine should be here any minute, along with the body guys from the coroner's office."

"You mean Hank and Ernie, don't you," Erin said heavily.

Webb nodded.

"I hate those guys," she said.

He nodded again.

*   *   *

Hank and Ernie drove the "meat wagon," the van which transported bodies to the Eightball's morgue. Ernie was tall and thin, Hank short and fat. They looked like the sort of dimwitted henchman who appeared in Disney movies. They survived their unpleasant job on a steady diet of pitch-black humor.

They arrived at about the same time as Sarah Levine, the Medical Examiner, meeting the detectives on the stairs outside the ballroom. Levine was less unpleasant than Hank and Ernie but no less odd. Levine was already wearing her gloves, scrubs, and lab coat when she got there. Erin had hardly ever seen her take them off.

"Where's the dead guy?" Levine asked.

"Girl," Vic said, pointing with his thumb. "She's in the fish tank."

Hank peered into the ballroom with interest. "It's an old Sicilian message," he said.

"She sleeps with the fishes," Ernie agreed solemnly.

"I hope they buy her breakfast afterward," Hank added. "She's not a mermaid. She's got legs."

"Nice ones," Ernie said. "That's always the problem with mermaids, y'know. Doesn't matter how nice she is up top. What're you supposed to do if you want to get some tail?"

"Get some tail," Hank repeated with a snicker.

"Stop ogling the victim," Webb said. "Anything you can tell us from the way she's presented, Doctor?"

Levine went in close to the aquarium and peered through the glass. "No obvious external signs of trauma," she said. "Pallor and blueness of lips and fingernails indicates possible asphyxiation."

"Hard to breathe under water," Ernie said.

"Was she dead before she went into the water?" Webb asked.

"I'll know when I do the autopsy," Levine said. "Two fingernails on the right hand appear to be broken off. Possible defensive wounds."

"Or she tried to claw her way out of the tank," Erin suggested. That was a nasty thought.

"If that's the case, the nails will be somewhere in the tank," Webb said. "Assuming the fish haven't eaten them."

"Do fish eat fingernails?" Erin asked.

"Do I look like an ichthyologist, O'Reilly?" Webb retorted. "That's a big tank, with a lot of water. We can't very well go through it looking for a couple of fingernails."

"That's unfortunate," Levine said. "It would be helpful to strain the water."

"We're not draining the tank," Webb said firmly. "The hotel won't let us. It'd kill the fish, for one thing."

"I like fish," Hank said. "Never eaten a regal blue tang before. How you think they taste?"

"Tangy," Ernie said.

"Okay, people," Webb said. "Let's get her out of there. Carefully."

"You know," Hank said thoughtfully, "sometimes when a body's been in the water a while, you reach out and grab it and pieces just come right off in your hands. The skin sloughs right off the bones and you're left with a skeleton."

"You lose any of her skin and I'll take a matching piece of yours," Vic said. "Skeletons. Jesus. What's the matter with you?"

"She's only been here a few hours, tops," Erin said. "I don't think it'll be a problem."

"She's right," Ernie said. "See, you can tell because of the bloating. The decomp gases start swelling up after a couple days and they blow up like balloons. Speaking of balloons..."

"Shut up," Webb, Erin, and Vic all said in unison.

*　　*　　*

While the coroner's squad worked on retrieving the body, the Major Crimes team went down to talk to the manager again. Feldspar had acquired a couple of associates in the meantime.

He was flanked by the hotel's chief of security and a lawyer. The security guy was a brawny, slightly overweight man with a buzzcut and a limp. The lawyer was a lawyer, which to Erin meant a weasel in an expensive suit.

"We don't need him," Webb said wearily, indicating the lawyer. "Your organization isn't being accused of anything, Mr. Feldspar. We just need to see your security tapes."

"There's an issue of privacy here, sir," the lawyer said.

"We don't need to see inside your guests' rooms," Webb said. "Or their bathrooms, or whatever."

"You don't have cameras inside the bathrooms, do you?" Vic asked, feigning surprise.

"No, we don't have bathroom cameras," Feldspar said, glaring at Vic.

"But the issue remains," the lawyer said.

"We're trying to identify the victim of a crime," Webb said. "We need to see footage from the hallway outside the maintenance door that accesses the aquarium. We also need to see any film you have from the charity dinner last night."

"That's the problem, gentlemen," the lawyer said, as if Erin wasn't standing right there. "Charity donors value their anonymity. We can't have them paraded before the press, or inveigled into a spurious police investigation."

"I'm just a dumb street cop," Vic said. "So I don't know what some of those words meant, but what I really don't understand is why an anonymous donor would show up to a fancy-dress dinner and show his face to everybody, and expect to stay anonymous. Can you explain that to me?"

"The hotel will be happy to comply with any legitimate court order you produce," the lawyer said.

"Mr. Feldspar," Webb said, ignoring the lawyer. "There's a dead young woman in your ballroom aquarium as we speak. She is either the victim of a tragic accident, a self-inflicted death, or a homicide. I can absolutely guarantee I can provide you with whatever documentation your lawyer requires, but it will take time. In that time, several things will happen, and one thing will not. What will happen is that a killer may have more time to cover his or her tracks; a young woman's friends and family will wonder and worry where she is; police officers, both in uniform and plainclothes, will continue to hang around your hotel and make your guests nervous; and your lawyer will bill you for every minute of the time he spends ostensibly looking after your interests. What will not happen is any sort of resolution. This whole thing will not just magically go away. Now, your lawyer is absolutely right. You can legally stall us until you get a court order. But is that really in anybody's best interest but his?"

Erin watched the lawyer's face as Webb talked. The man's mouth slowly tightened and his lips compressed until she wondered if he was about to implode. She gave a sidelong look to Vic and saw he was doing the same thing she was, which was trying to hide a smile. Webb could be unpleasant sometimes, but it was a beautiful thing watching him take someone apart using nothing but words.

"Barry, please take these detectives to the security station and give them whatever assistance they need," Feldspar said to the security man.

"Sure thing, boss," Barry said. "After me, folks."

Chapter 3

Erin's least favorite part of being a detective was the paperwork, but watching security footage was a close second. She'd rather be hosing vomit out of the back of her squad car. That was messier, but at least it was over quickly. Unfortunately, she didn't have a choice, so she was now playing hunt-the-pixel in a grainy video feed, trying to pick out a particular young woman from a crowd of well-dressed dinner guests. Next to her, Vic was doing pretty much the same thing with the upstairs hallway footage.

She'd hoped the victim's age and attractiveness would make her stand out, but she quickly saw that many of the philanthropists at the dinner were older guys with trophy wives, girlfriends, or mistresses. All the arm-candy looked virtually identical to her. She had to keep rubbing her eyes and blinking to refocus.

Rolf settled himself beside her chair, rested his chin on his paws, and went to sleep, showing once again that he was the smartest member of the Major Crimes squad. Webb drifted back and forth between Erin and Vic, looking over their shoulders and contributing nothing.

Finally, after twenty minutes of monochrome "Where's Waldo," Erin saw what she was looking for. At the table in the lower left of the camera's field of view, a woman who'd been seated with her back to the camera leaned over to say something to her date. He faced her to reply and Erin got a good look at both faces in profile.

"I got her, sir," she said, pausing the video.

Webb was beside her in an instant. "Where?"

"There." She pointed.

"Looks like her," he agreed. "Hey, Barry?"

"Yeah?" the security man asked, setting down the cup of coffee he'd been sipping.

"Did this dinner have a seating chart?"

"I think so. Let me check." He sat down at his computer and scrolled through his files. "Okay, yeah, I got it here."

"Who's at this table?" Webb asked, pointing to the screen.

Barry squinted at the monitor. "Jeez, this resolution is crap."

"It's your machine, not ours," Webb said sourly.

"You think I buy the equipment?" Barry returned just as sourly. "My Aunt Edna could be there and I wouldn't recognize her. Useless piece of junk. Okay, that's table five, I think. Going by the orientation that's, um, Stone. Wendell J Stone. The third."

"Sounds like a rich asshole," Vic said without looking away from his own monitor.

"Neshenko," Webb said warningly.

"A rich, charitable asshole," Vic corrected.

"And who's the girl sitting next to him?" Erin asked.

"Hell if I know," Barry said.

"She crashed the party?"

"No, but the invite was for Stone and a plus-one. Like a wedding invitation. He could've brought anyone."

"So she's not Stone's wife?" Webb asked.

"She look like his wife?" Barry replied. "You ask me, that girl's a pro."

"You get many prostitutes here?" Erin asked. "If you can pick them out of a crowd, you must."

Barry gave her a cynical smile. "Detective, I worked Vice for four years before I landed this gig."

"You're too young to be pensioned off," she said. "What happened?"

"Partial disability. Messed up my knee in a fight with a pimp. He cracked the cap with a tire iron."

"Ouch," she said with a sympathetic wince. "You know Tad Brown? Vice Sergeant down at the Eight?"

"Yeah, I know Brown. I worked a couple busts with him back in the day. He made Sergeant, huh? Good for him. Tell him Caldwell says hi."

"I'll do that," Erin said with a smile. She was glad to hear Barry had been one of their own. "Why do you say this girl's a hooker?"

"Hotel policy is to keep 'em out," he said, rolling his eyes. "But everybody knows they get in. And what're you gonna do? Ask to see a marriage license? What we mostly get are high-class call girls. Our clients have plenty of cash to sling around, so they go for the good ones. As long as nobody causes trouble, I don't get involved. I like having a job, y'know? But I know the look. I'd say she's working for an escort service, sure."

"Great," Erin muttered. That could make the victim very hard to identify. "I guess we can always check Missing Persons."

"This Stone," Webb said. "Is he local, or is he staying at the InterContinental?"

"Just a sec," Barry said, returning to his computer and bringing up the guest list. "Hey, looks like you hit the jackpot, Lieutenant. He's staying here, all right. Last night and tonight."

"I suppose it's too much to ask for him to be in his room right now," Webb said. "Which room is it?"

"503," Barry said. "Listen, sir, I don't wanna make any trouble for you, but could you try not to make any for me? You start hassling the guests, Mr. Feldspar's gonna come down on me hard. You really need to talk to this guy?"

"He's one of the last people to see our victim alive," Webb said. "We have to talk to him. But I'll be polite."

"I won't," Vic said.

"Then you can stay here and keep going over the footage while O'Reilly and I go upstairs," Webb said.

"Walked right into that, didn't I," Vic said gloomily.

"Like stepping in a big pile of fresh dogshit," Erin agreed. "Rolf. *Komm!*"

The Shepherd was immediately awake and on his paws, ready to go to work. Maybe chasing and biting would be back on the agenda.

* * *

"You and Neshenko getting on better?" Webb asked Erin on the elevator ride.

"I think so," Erin said. She couldn't tell him that Vic was still pissed off at her for hiding her relationship with Carlyle. Hell, he was pissed at her for being in the relationship at all. But he'd tumbled to the fact that Carlyle was now cooperating against the O'Malleys, which at least meant he recognized they were all more or less playing for the same team. Unfortunately, Webb wasn't in on the secret, which meant he couldn't know anything about it for reasons of operational security.

"I don't really care," Webb said. "I just care that you can work together."

"We can, sir," Erin replied. "You're all heart."

"I have to be," he said. "The cigarettes wiped out my lungs. Heart is all I've got left."

They got out on the fifth floor and went to the door marked 503. Erin leaned her head close to the wood.

"TV's on," she said quietly.

"Good," Webb said. "Someone's home." He knocked.

After a moment, the sound of the television was muted. The detectives waited.

The door opened, which Erin found to be a pleasant change of pace. Often, in police work, people shouted at you through a closed door, or opened it but kept the chain-lock engaged. But this was a fancy hotel in a good part of town, and apparently the man in 503 didn't feel endangered. He stood there, gray-haired, distinguished, with a neatly trimmed goatee and mustache, wearing what could only be described as a smoking jacket. Dark red and made of silk, it was nicer than any dress Erin owned.

"Good morning, sir," the man said to Webb. His accent was more Boston than New York, saying his Rs like Hs. "Ma'am," he added, glancing at Erin. Then he caught sight of Rolf and blinked. "I think perhaps you have the wrong room."

Webb held up his shield. "Lieutenant Webb, NYPD," he said. "This is Detective O'Reilly. Are you Wendell Stone?"

"Wendell Jeremy Stone the Third, at your service," he said. "I don't know what possible interest New York's finest could have in me."

"We just need to ask you a few questions," Webb said, employing the classic detective line. "May we come in?"

"I'm hardly equipped for entertaining," he said. "But certainly. It's better than standing chattering in the hall. Your police dog... I presume he's well trained?"

"He's a working K-9, sir," Erin said. "He's better trained than the rookies we get from the Academy."

Stone laughed. "Very well then, Miss... O'Reilly, was it? Do come in. I'm charmed to meet you."

He offered his hand, on which was a Harvard class ring. Erin and Webb shook. Then Stone got down on one knee and solemnly offered his hand to Rolf.

Rolf just stared at him. Then he looked at Erin for instruction.

"He never learned to shake," she explained to Stone. "He's better at sniffing out bombs and biting perps."

Stone's room was luxuriously furnished in white and gold. All the furniture looked high-class and expensive. Erin was afraid to touch anything. She stood in the middle of the room, looking for anything out of place. The TV was still on but muted, showing some sort of boring business broadcast with serious-looking guys in suits and stock prices on the screen. The bed was rumpled and unmade. She saw only one pillow with an indentation in it.

"You attended a charity function here last night," Webb said.

"That's correct," Stone said. "Would you care for something to drink? It's early for anything strong, but the minibar here is well-stocked with softer beverages. Orange juice, perhaps? It came up from room service, fresh-squeezed. It's really very good."

"No, thank you," Webb said. "Your invitation was for you and one guest. Did you bring a companion?"

"Yes."

"Are you married, Mr. Stone?"

Stone laughed. "Alas, I haven't yet encountered the proper lady to bring Wendell Jeremy Stone the Fourth into this world. I remain unencumbered by matrimony."

Erin had already noted that, aside from the class ring on his right hand, Stone's fingers were bare. But that didn't mean anything. Plenty of married guys didn't wear wedding rings, especially if they were hanging out with other women.

"Who was your guest?" Erin asked.

"A charming young lady of my acquaintance," Stone said.

"What's her name?"

"She was introduced to me as Miss Crystal Winters."

"Crystal Winters," Webb repeated, deadpan.

"I shouldn't wonder if her birth name was something different," Stone allowed. "But that is the one I was given."

"How did you meet Miss Winters?" Webb asked.

"I encountered her at a similar function to the one last night."

"She was a guest at a charity dinner?"

"Not a guest, precisely. That function included a display of women's swimwear. Miss Winters wore a lovely aquamarine bikini and I must say, she wore it exceptionally well. I introduced myself to her after the show."

I'll bet you did, Erin thought. What she said was, "Were you romantically involved with Miss Winters?"

Stone cleared his throat. "Ah, not precisely."

"What modeling agency was she working through?" Webb asked.

"Ethereal Angels."

"What happened after dinner last night?" Erin asked.

"After dinner?" Stone repeated. "Dessert, of course. A delicious baked Alaska."

"And after that?"

"After that, we retired to my room for some quiet conversation and refreshment."

"When did she leave?"

"About, oh, I should say eleven o' clock. Detective, whatever on Earth is this about? Is Miss Winters in some sort of trouble?"

"She's dead," Erin said, being deliberately blunt, watching him for a reaction.

"Dead? Oh, my." Stone blinked. "Oh, that poor girl. And she seemed so healthy and energetic. However did it happen?"

"Did Miss Winters act at all strange?" Webb asked. "Was she frightened? Upset?"

"No, nothing of the sort," Stone said. "She was her usual charming self. Although..."

"Yes?" Webb and Erin said in unison, pouncing on the word.

"She was rather... how shall I say it..." Stone hesitated. "I don't wish to speak ill of the dead, Detectives. And I don't wish to disparage a woman's reputation. But she was rather on edge. Jittery. As if she'd ingested or perhaps injected something which was affecting her."

"Are you saying she was using drugs?" Erin asked.

"I'm hardly an authority in the field," Stone said. "But the thought crossed my mind."

"How much alcohol did she drink?" Erin knew that combining alcohol with hard drugs could have unpredictable and nasty effects.

"A cocktail and some wine with dinner," Stone said, rubbing his goatee. "And then three of those little bottles from the bar in my room. Oh dear. She didn't try to drive in an impaired condition, did she?"

"We can't discuss the details," Webb said. "So, she left here at eleven? Was anyone with her?"

"No," Stone said. "I stayed up watching television a short while longer, then went to sleep. And here I have remained. I'm sorry I can't be more assistance, but I really don't know what happened to her after that."

Erin gave him one of her cards. "If you think of anything else, please call me."

"You'll be the first to know, young lady," he said with a smile. "Are you married, by any chance?"

"Sir, that's not relevant," she said.

"I'm terribly sorry. I didn't mean to be rude."

Erin gave him a bland smile. On the scale of rudeness an NYPD officer dealt with, Wendell J Stone III hardly registered.

"Thank you for your time, Mr. Stone," Webb said. "How long are you planning to be in town?"

"I shall be returning to Boston tomorrow evening."

"Flying?"

"I prefer to travel by rail. It has a more civilized feel, don't you agree?"

"Whatever gets me where I'm going is fine with me," Webb said. "Good day, sir."

* * *

"Pretentious jerk," Erin muttered once they were back in the elevator.

"In my experience, money doesn't make jerks," Webb said. "But lots of jerks make money. Street corners or Wall Street, it's all the same."

"That's almost poetic, sir."

They walked back to the security office. From the hallway they could hear Vic's voice. Erin couldn't quite make out the words, but he sounded angry.

"Uh oh," she said, jogging the last few steps and throwing open the door.

"What do you mean, you don't know?" Vic shouted.

"I mean I don't know!" Barry shouted back. "I'm not sitting here twenty-four seven, okay? I don't know what the hell goes on when I'm not in the office!"

"You're in charge of security!" Vic yelled. "You damn well oughta know! It's your job to know!"

"What the hell's going on here?" Webb demanded, hurrying in on Erin's heels.

"This jackoff," Vic said, indicating Barry with a contemptuous thumb, "doesn't know what happened to the footage."

"What footage?" Webb asked.

"I'm missing half an hour of hallway footage from last night. I checked the time stamps and there's a gap."

"When?" Erin asked.

"Eleven-thirty to midnight."

"I assume you didn't find anything on the rest of the tape?" Webb asked.

"Of course not," Vic growled.

"Look," Barry said. "Let me check the maintenance logs. Maybe something happened. An electrical glitch or something. That happens sometimes."

"Pretty damn convenient electrical glitch," Vic said. "Right in the middle of our time window."

"Convenient," Erin agreed. "Check the log, would you, Barry?"

"Working on it," the security man said. "Look, guys, this isn't my fault, okay? I don't mean to get you jammed up."

"And yet here we are," Vic said. "Jammed up. Listen, I don't care if it's your fault. It's your responsibility and it went wrong."

"Take it easy, Neshenko," Webb said. "We're all trying to solve this thing."

As Barry went back to his computer, Erin stepped up beside Vic and whispered, "This is why you don't get to be good cop in the interrogation room."

"Sometimes I think we got nothing but bad cops," Vic muttered.

"Looks like we had a fuse go at eleven-thirty," Barry reported. "It didn't take out power to the whole hotel, just the third floor. Maintenance was called and they got on it right away, but it took a few minutes to sort it out."

Webb rubbed his temples. "Okay. I guess we do this the hard way, then. Thanks for the help, Caldwell. Here's my card. Give me a call if you find anything else."

"Now what, sir?" Erin asked.

"Levine should have our victim back to the morgue soon," he said. "In the meantime, it's unlikely anyone saw anything, but I'd like the two of you to knock on doors. Maybe we'll get lucky and someone was out in the hallway getting ice or something. Neshenko, try the fifth floor and the third floor. O'Reilly, talk to the staff."

"If they're on duty now, they probably weren't last night," she pointed out.

"Then find out who was on duty so we have a list of names," he said. "If you can get anything, it'll be more than we have now."

Chapter 4

Erin was right about the staff. None of the bellhops, maids, or other hotel employees she tracked down had been on duty the previous night. She returned to the front desk and got Feldspar to put together a list of the people who'd been working. It was a depressingly long list, but the InterContinental was a large hotel. They'd need to come back in the evening to catch the overnight workers. The only name she recognized from the list was Barry Caldwell.

"If he was working last night, what was he doing here this morning?" she asked Feldspar.

"I called him when Rosa found the... when she found... you know, *it*. He got here right after you."

"Have you had any problems with any of the people on this list?" she asked.

"What sort of problems?"

"Things going missing? Any shady activities?"

Feldspar raised his eyebrows. "Detective, if I'd suspected any of these people of anything of the sort, I would have fired them immediately. Do you think I would keep a thief on the payroll? This is a respectable hotel."

"So nothing out of the ordinary?"

"Nothing illegal. That is... nothing that would concern your department."

Erin caught the hesitation. "What do you mean?"

Feldspar glanced to either side. "Detective, every major hotel in New York does it. You know it's true. With housing and labor costs what they are, you understand we may not completely vet the, ah, credentials of everyone we employ, particularly in the housekeeping and laundry departments."

"I understand," Erin said. Feldspar was saying the hotel employed undocumented workers. And he was right, it was a very common practice. It was technically illegal, but only the folks at Immigration really seemed to care. Erin herself didn't. She viewed her job as catching criminals, which in her book was people who preyed on other people, not poor folks who'd come to New York hoping to find a better life. Her own ancestors had come from Ireland for the same reason.

"Good," Feldspar said, looking relieved.

"If you do think of anything," she said, producing a business card, "you'll let me know?"

"Certainly." He sighed. "This is all very unpleasant, not to mention inconvenient."

Erin didn't bother to answer that. She left him standing there at the front desk and went looking for Webb.

She and Rolf found him in the ballroom, looking at the aquarium. The fish tank was now empty except for the fish.

"They get the body out okay?" she asked.

"Yeah," he said. "Levine said she'd get on the autopsy right away. We should have the results by the end of the day, tomorrow morning at the latest. In the meantime, I want you to run down this Angel-Whatever modeling company and see if you can get an ID on our girl."

"Ethereal Angels," she said.

"Ethereal," Webb repeated. "I think that means ghostly, or maybe angelic. I hope you know how to spell it, because I've got no idea."

*   *   *

Erin used the computer in her Charger to look up Ethereal Angels. It didn't link to any known criminal activity, but that didn't surprise her. Fronts for prostitution changed identities constantly. She found a website which appeared to be aboveboard, but that might just be window-dressing. She hoped to establish the company's bona fides before talking to them. And that meant talking to someone from Vice.

She drove back to the Eightball and went up to the Vice office. It was a converted supply closet, windowless and stuffy. She and Rolf found the Vice Sergeant at his desk. He was examining a strange tangle of black leather straps and buckles.

"Hey there, Brown," she said, knocking on the door.

Tad Brown looked up. He was a heavyset cop with a face and body prematurely aged by bad food and cynicism. Most cops had a dim view of human nature; Sergeant Brown's was midnight black. When he saw Erin, his face approximated a smile.

"If it isn't the Major Crimes attack dog," he said. "And her pooch. Say, can I ask you something?"

"Shoot."

"You're a woman, right?"

"Last time I checked."

"Then it's two questions, actually." He held up the leather contraption. "How would you wear this, and why is it sexy?"

Erin looked at it. "Brown, I've got no idea what the hell that is. And if you think I'm trying it on for you, I'd rather Tase myself in the tongue."

"Now *that* might be sexy, for some guys. You name it, there's a fetish for it. What's up, O'Reilly? Nobody ever comes here just to make small talk."

"A couple things," she said. "First off, we caught a Jane Doe. Probable homicide. Young woman, no ID. She was an older guy's date last night at a charity dinner."

"Classic," Brown said. "Guys think donating to charity gets the ladies interested in them."

"She turned up dead this morning, floating in an aquarium. We tracked down her date."

"How'd you manage that?"

"Security footage from the dinner. He says her name's Crystal Winters, but that's probably not real. He got in touch with her through a modeling company called Ethereal Angels."

"Prostitution front," Brown said immediately.

"You know them?"

"Nope. But they're all prostitution fronts."

"You can't possibly mean that."

"I mean it," Brown said. "Because everybody's a whore. You, me, everyone. It's just a question of what we sell, and to whom."

"Can the philosophy, Brown. I need to know about Ethereal Angels, because they're my best bet on finding out who this girl really was. You got anything on them at all?"

He shook his head. "Doesn't ring any bells. Are they new?"

"I don't know."

Brown stared at his computer screen. "Where do they operate?"

"Manhattan."

"Okay, that's not an alias for any call-girl ring I know of," he said. "That doesn't mean they're clean. They may be more careful than most, or just luckier. Sorry, Detective. I got bubkis."

Erin nodded. "Thanks anyway."

"You said there was something else?" he prompted.

"Yeah. Barry Caldwell says hi."

Brown looked surprised. "Where the hell did you run into Caldwell? I haven't seen him since he turned in his shield."

"He runs security at a hotel now. Sounds like you knew him?"

"Yeah. He was on Vice for a few years, back in the day." Brown sat back in his chair, remembering. A frown crossed his face.

"What?" Erin asked.

"Nothing."

"Something I should know about him?"

"It's old news, O'Reilly. Even if you were Internal Affairs it wouldn't matter anymore."

"Was he into something?" she asked.

"Nothing big. You know the difference between clean graft and dirty graft?"

Erin felt her jaw tighten. She'd heard this from her dad once, when she was a kid.

"If you put on a shield, kiddo," he'd said, *"sometime you're going to get an offer. Someone's going to offer you money, or favors, or a new watch, or whatever. And they'll tell you it's okay, because it's clean graft. There's a difference between clean graft and dirty graft. Clean graft is taking a payoff to let a bookie run numbers. It's letting a guy skate on a parking ticket. The cops who take it think it's okay because it's small potatoes. Dirty graft comes from murderers and drug dealers. But here's the thing, kiddo. If you take clean graft, you're on the take just as bad as if you take dirty. And you'll have to live with that, and someday you'll have to square it."*

"Caldwell was on the take," she said.

"I didn't say that."

"You didn't have to."

"He tell you how he got that limp?"

"Yeah. Pimp with a tire iron."

Brown chuckled mirthlessly. "Yeah, that part's true. Did he tell you why that pimp laid into him?"

"He left that part out."

"Yeah, that's because he was leaning on the pimp for protection and the guy didn't like his attitude. Caldwell figured he was safe because no one would take a shot at a guy wearing a shield. He wasn't creative enough to see there's a whole lot of things you can do to a guy short of shooting him."

"What happened to the pimp?"

Brown shrugged. "Five to ten for assaulting an officer. He's probably back on the street by now, doing the same old business."

"Thanks for the help, Brown."

"Don't mention it."

"You ever take clean graft?" The question just popped out.

"O'Reilly, I've been wearing a shield eighteen years. Twelve of those I've been working Vice. Nothing you see on Vice is clean. And I've gotten plenty dirty without it."

"Credit to the force, Brown."

"You too, O'Reilly. But then, you'd know more about this than I do."

Erin paused on her way out of the office. "Come again?"

"Clean graft."

She felt simultaneously hot and cold as anger and unease rushed through her. "I don't know what you've heard, Brown..." she began.

He held up a hand. "Yeah, I know, it's not like that. It never is. It's kind of comforting, actually. I thought you were different, maybe, but no one's above it. You grab what you can in this world, because it gets dark outside. I get it."

He knew about Carlyle. Or maybe he didn't know that, exactly, but he knew something. Rumors were flying around the Eightball. Erin gritted her teeth. It actually helped her undercover operation if guys like Brown thought she was dirty, but it was infuriating.

"You think what you want," she said. "Hell, you'll do that anyway." And she left, but not in a good mood.

* * *

Erin went up to the Major Crimes office and took a seat at her desk. Rolf curled up in his spot next to it and watched her. When she picked up her phone, he settled himself for a snooze.

She called the number on the Ethereal Angels website and prepared for an automated menu, or maybe a long hold time.

To her pleasant surprise, she got a human being immediately. The voice didn't belong to someone she pictured working for an escort service. It was a guy with a Brooklyn accent.

"Ethereal Angels," he said, like he was saying the name of a motorcycle gang. "What can I do for ya?"

"My name is Detective O'Reilly," she said. "I'm with the NYPD. Can I talk to your boss?"

"NYPD, huh? Bullshit. Nice try."

"You want bullshit?" Erin retorted. "How about when I come to your office and haul your ass downtown for obstructing my investigation?"

"Uh, just a second," he said.

There was a short pause. Then another voice, smoother, older, and more businesslike, came on the line.

"Detective?"

"This is Detective O'Reilly. Who am I talking to?"

"Nolan Copeland. I'm the owner of Ethereal Angels. What can I do for you?"

"I need to talk to you about one of your models."

"Oh, dear. Should I engage the services of a lawyer?"

"We don't need one, unless you've been doing something you shouldn't. This is about Crystal Winters."

"Ah, yes, I know the young lady. I hope she's not in some sort of trouble."

"What's her real name?"

There was a short pause. "Detective," Copeland said, "I don't understand. Surely Ms. Winters can provide you with that information herself."

"I'm afraid not," Erin said.

"Ah." There was another pause. "I take it Ms. Winters is in no condition to respond to your inquiries?"

"That's correct."

Copeland sighed. "Her name is Sarah Devers. I'm afraid I only really know her in her professional capacity."

"Meaning what, exactly?"

"She's a quite lovely young woman with a fine sense for the camera, good poise, excellent posture, and remarkable bone structure. I had hopes she'll go far with our organization. But now I think you're about to tell me something has happened to her."

"Can you think of any reason anyone would do something to her?"

"No, Detective, I can't. Sarah is a beautiful girl. I can't imagine anyone would want to harm her."

"Did she have any problems with drugs or alcohol?"

"Of course not!" Copeland sounded shocked. "She's only seventeen, Detective, and I require all my models to take regular substance tests. She's never returned a positive result on any drug test."

"Did she have any bad experience with anyone? At a photoshoot, maybe?"

"No. Detective, please tell me. Is she all right?"

"Sir, she's dead."

"What? When?"

"Last night."

"That's terrible! How... that is, what happened?"

"That's what we're working on finding out. Do you know where she was last night?"

"No. She wasn't working. I don't keep tabs on my employees in their downtime."

"Do you know if she was seeing anyone? A boyfriend, maybe?"

Copeland paused. "Yes, she was dating a young man."

Erin caught the word. "A young man, you said? Not an older guy?"

"No. One of our photographers. I don't encourage that sort of thing. It leads to favoritism and can compromise their work, and if they have friction, they bring it to work with them, but it does happen."

"Who's the guy?"

"Randy Schilling. He didn't have anything to do with this, did he?"

"Do you know where he was last night?"

"We had an afternoon shoot uptown. He was there."

"How long did it run?"

"We finished shooting right after the sun went down. Then we had dinner on site. I guess he left after dinner. Say, about eight."

"Do you have a phone number and address for Schilling?"

"Of course." He gave her the numbers. "But I can't imagine he would have done anything to Sarah. He seemed very... fond of her."

Erin heard the hesitation. "Except?" she prompted.

"Well, there were some suspicions that Randy might be making use of some controlled substances. Unfortunately, we don't currently require substance tests from our photographers, only our models. And he's been exhibiting some unpredictable behavior recently. I've been meaning to talk to him about it. I think it may have been affecting his relationship with Sarah as well."

Erin felt a surge of excitement. "I need to talk to him," she said. "As soon as possible. Is he in your office now?"

"No, but he's due in this afternoon at two o' clock. We're doing another afternoon shoot."

"I'll be there at two. Don't let him leave."

Chapter 5

Erin called Webb from her car, on the way to the modeling agency.

"Give me good news," he said.

"Drug-addict boyfriend?"

"Good enough for me. What do you know about him?"

"He's a photographer for the modeling agency."

"I like him already," Webb said. "What else have you got?"

"Her real name is Sarah Devers. She was seventeen."

"So, this boyfriend. Suppose he follows her on her dinner date with Stone, sees the two of them, gets jealous..."

"That's what I was thinking," Erin said. "Or it could've been an accident. Maybe he saw her after she left Stone's room and gave her a little pick-me-up. The owner of the agency said she was clean, but that might mean she didn't know her limits and took too much."

"Could be. But then how did she end up in the aquarium? What do you want to do next?"

"I'm going to the agency to brace the boyfriend."

"Sounds good. Neshenko and I are still interviewing people at the InterContinental. It's hit-or-miss, but you never know. I told Levine to prioritize cause of death and bloodwork. We should know what killed her by the end of the day."

*   *   *

Erin was expecting the Ethereal Angels office to be something sleazy, maybe a strip-mall storefront. What she got was an office in a Manhattan high-rise. She checked some of the other company names in the building while she and Rolf waited for the elevator. The modeling agency shared their building with a realtor, a chiropractor, and a couple of CPAs, to pick a few. The lobby was clean and well-kept. If this was a front for prostitution, it was definitely one of the higher-end operations.

She got off on the twelfth floor and walked down a hallway to a door labeled ETHEREAL ANGELS. On the door was a photo of a gorgeous young woman's face, the lower half hidden by white feathers, staring at Erin with a pair of fantastically blue eyes. Erin opened the door and went in, Rolf keeping time beside her.

A big, square-jawed guy was sitting behind the counter. He gave her an appraising look and nodded.

"Okay," he said. "Not bad. You got the bone structure. A little older than we usually go for, but looks like you got a decent bod. I'll get you an application and a waiver. We got a photographer who just came in, he can do a sample set. If you got a portfolio, I'll take it. The dog a prop, or an assistance animal, or what?"

"He's a police K-9," Erin said, showing her shield. "And I'm not here to pose. O'Reilly, Major Crimes. We spoke on the phone a little while ago."

He looked startled. "Oh. Right, yeah. Mr. Copeland said you might be dropping in. Sorry about the mix-up. I didn't mean nothing by it. But you got the looks. If we'd caught you when you were eighteen, we could get you some swimsuit work maybe—"

"Thanks," she said, letting the sarcasm drip off the word. "Where's Randy Schilling?"

"He just got here. He's prepping his equipment. Studio Three." The receptionist jerked a thumb over his shoulder.

Erin led Rolf to the indicated door. She tried the door and it opened.

She found herself in a dimly-lit room. On her right were several racks loaded with all sorts of women's clothing, from undergarments all the way to winter coats. On her left was an open space, the wall and floor smooth and painted a bright, uniform green. Big lights were pointed toward the space, each sporting a backing of reflective silver to amplify their effect. At the moment they weren't lit.

Rolf sniffed the air and pulled slightly to the right, toward the clothing. Erin angled that direction. As she walked into the room, she heard two voices; one male, one female.

"You're gonna see, babe," the male voice said. "I am gonna make you look so hot."

"I bet you say that to every girl," the female voice replied, giving a giggle that grated on Erin's ear.

"Nah, babe, not every girl is Sports Illustrated material. I'm talking swimsuit edition. Legs like yours... man oh man."

Erin stepped around a rack of Japanese kimonos and saw the two speakers. The guy had the girl up against the wall and was touching her face with one hand. His other was sliding up one of the legs he'd been talking about. The girl was wearing a white bikini. Their faces were only a couple of inches apart.

Erin cleared her throat. "Randy Schilling?" she prompted.

The guy jumped and the girl gave a little cry of surprise. He spun around and Erin saw a face that was good-looking in a rough sort of way, a face that looked right with the layer of stubble and slightly disheveled hair framing it. He was dressed in jeans and a button-down shirt under a leather jacket. A camera was slung over his shoulder.

"What the hell?" he said by way of greeting. Erin reflected that interrupting a horny guy making time with a girl was guaranteed to piss him off.

"NYPD," she said, flashing her shield.

The girl giggled again. "Oh Randy, we are so busted."

"What the hell do you want?" Schilling demanded. "I'm kinda busy here."

"Yeah, I can see that," Erin said. "And I hate to interrupt. But we need to talk about your girlfriend."

"What the hell are you talking about?"

"Sarah Devers," she said. "Unless you've forgotten about her already."

"What the hell does she have to do with anything?"

Erin wondered whether he started all his sentences the same way. "When's the last time you saw Sarah?"

"What the hell business is that of yours?" he retorted, answering her internal question in the affirmative.

"I'm a detective with Major Crimes," she said. "That makes Miss Devers my business."

"*So* busted," the girl in the bikini repeated.

"Whatever the hell you got on her, it's got nothing to do with me," Schilling said. "Shove off."

"Sir," Erin said firmly, "I'm going to need you to tell me where you were last night between eleven and two."

"Bite me, bitch. Get outta here."

"Good choice of words, Mr. Schilling," Erin said with a smile. "I'd like you to meet my partner. This is Rolf. He's a trained K-9. He'll be happy to bite you. And he won't let go until I tell him to, no matter what you do to him. Now, we can do this with or without teeth. Your choice."

Schilling hadn't noticed the dark-pattern German Shepherd, who'd been partially hidden by the clothes rack. Now he
did.

"You can't do that," he said.

"I don't *want* to," Erin corrected. "Rolf, on the other hand? *He*
wants to. Now, where were you? Last night, after you left
supper?"

"I went to a bar. A couple bars. Had a few drinks."

"How many?"

"I dunno. Didn't keep track."

"Did you take anything else? Speed? A little coke, maybe?"

Schilling glared at her and said nothing. The swimsuit
model giggled and rubbed her nose.

"Did anyone see you at these bars?"

"Yeah, I guess. The bartenders."

"What were the names?"

"How the hell do I know that? They're bartenders. They're
not my friends. I don't know these guys."

"Not the bartenders, wiseass. The bars."

"I don't remember."

"Where did you go after you left the last bar?"

"I dunno. Walked around a bit, then I went home."

"When did you leave?"

"I dunno."

"*That's* your story? You went to a couple of bars you don't
remember, alone, and then you went home at some time or
other? That's the worst alibi I've ever heard, and that's saying
something."

Schilling shrugged. "What the hell do I need an alibi for? I
didn't do nothing."

"Why were you fighting with Sarah?" Erin demanded,
shifting topics with deliberate speed to throw him off.

"I wasn't fighting with her!"

"That's not what I heard."

"Who the hell told you that?"

"Doesn't matter how I know," Erin said. "Were you fighting about this girl here? Or another girl?"

"I have a name," the girl said. "It's Tawny. Well, that's my working name. My real name's Nicole."

Neither Erin nor Schilling was listening to her. Tawny pouted. They didn't notice that either.

"She was riding me," Schilling said sullenly. "About... some shit I was doing. Come on, it's not like we were exclusive or nothing. She didn't have no right to tell me what to do."

"I bet she wouldn't leave you alone," Erin said, nodding.

"Mouthy bitch wouldn't shut up," Schilling agreed.

"But you showed her who was boss," Erin said. "I get it, a man's got to do that sometimes. Otherwise he's just whipped."

"Yeah," Schilling said. "I had to show her a thing or two. Girl didn't understand nothing. Comes from some hick town and thinks she's gonna be famous, like her shit don't stink. So she's pretty. Pretty faces are everywhere. You turn around, you trip over a pretty face. No goddamn homecoming queen can just waltz into New York and be famous. It don't work like that. And she thinks she's better than me? Screw that, and screw her. I don't need that in my life."

Erin kept nodding. "So you shut her up."

"Yeah."

"And then you stuffed her in the fish tank."

Schilling nodded. Then he blinked. "Wait, what?"

"The aquarium. At the hotel," Erin said patiently.

"What the hell are you talking about?"

"You killed her and dumped her in the aquarium."

"Sarah's *dead*?"

"That's what happens when you're stuck underwater all night. One question, Randy. Was she dead before she went into the water, or did you just slam the lid and let her drown?"

"You're crazy! I didn't do nothing!"

"You just told me you shut her up, Randy. I suppose you want me to believe you gave her a kiss on the cheek and a glass of warm milk?" Erin pulled out her cuffs. "Turn around and put your hands behind your back."

"Ooh," Tawny said. "Kinky."

"This is nuts!" Schilling said. Then he moved. He was fast, lunging at Erin.

Crooks never understood. Cops put cuffs on guys all the time. They'd seen the tricks. She was ready for him. She didn't know whether he was trying to fight her, or to push past and make a run for it, but it didn't matter. He put out an arm and shoved at her. She grabbed the extended arm, used her hip as a pivot, and tossed him in a judo throw. Schilling made a short, surprised flight through the air that ended when his back smacked into the clothes rack. He went down in a clatter of coat-hangers and kimonos.

Rolf, hackles standing on end, barked excitedly. He wanted in on the action.

"Stay down," Erin warned Schilling.

But Schilling had just been humiliated in front of a girl he'd been trying to impress and he wasn't badly hurt. He came up with a roar of fury, hands reaching for Erin's throat.

"*Fass!*" Erin ordered.

Rolf sprang. His teeth snapped shut on Schilling's right arm.

The man's roar turned into a wail of surprise and pain. He went down again, dragged to the floor by ninety pounds of muscle, fur, and teeth. This time he stayed there.

*   *   *

Webb and Vic hurried back to the Eightball, arriving just as Erin was finishing booking Schilling. She left him in the interrogation room and met her fellow detectives in the observation room next door. Webb was amused and Vic was annoyed.

"You gotta have all the fun without me?" Vic demanded.

"Wasn't that much fun," Erin said. "He jumped me, Rolf and I took him down. You want, I can have Rolf bite you, too, and you can see what you missed."

"I'll pass." Vic had helped train Rolf before. He had no desire to put the bite suit back on.

"We haven't even ruled it a homicide yet," Webb said. He was smiling. "And you already busted a perp. That's got to be a new record for closure, solving a crime before it's officially a crime. You sure he's our guy?"

"He practically confessed to it," Erin said. "The only thing is, he seemed surprised about the aquarium."

"How do you mean?" Webb asked. His smile vanished.

"I was leading him just fine through a confession. He admitted to beating our victim up, admitted he was mad at her. Classic crime-of-passion stuff. But he didn't seem to know how we found her."

"If I killed a girl that way, I'd remember it," Vic said.

"I'd hope you'd remember whoever you killed," Erin said.

"I didn't mean it like that. I mean, the way she looked in that tank was eerie as hell. Just floating there like that. I'm gonna have nightmares about it."

"Just drink until you can't remember," she suggested. "You know, Schilling said he had some drinks. You think maybe he blacked out some of the evening?"

"Could be," Vic agreed. "And maybe he had some more after, to forget."

"If we could put the alcohol abuse on hold for a few more hours?" Webb said. "Neshenko's right. It's strange he wouldn't know how the body was found, but maybe not impossible. If he was at the hotel, and somehow got access to that back room, he might've just thought he was stashing the body somewhere out of the way. If he was never in the ballroom, he might not have known what it'd look like. Or he might've had an accomplice at the hotel. We have too many unknowns right now."

"So let's interrogate him," Erin said. "Find out what else he knows."

"Take it easy, O'Reilly," Webb said, pointing at the one-way mirror that showed the adjoining room. "Look at him."

Schilling was drumming his feet and hands. If he hadn't been cuffed in place, Erin was sure he would have been pacing the room.

"He's restless," she said. "Edgy."

"Exactly," Webb said. "And it sounds like he's impulsive. A guy like that, if we leave him to stew for a while, who knows what he might spill? He's not going anywhere. We've got him cold on assaulting an officer, so that's plenty to hold him. Put him in holding overnight. We'll take a run at him first thing in the morning. I'm guessing he won't get much sleep, and that'll make it even easier."

"What do we do in the meantime?" Erin asked.

"Unless I'm mistaken, O'Reilly, you've got some DD-5s to fill out. And the arrest report, of course. And..."

"I get the idea, sir," Erin sighed. She'd had her fun. Now it was time to pay for it.

"You oughta teach Rolf to read and write," Vic snickered. "Then he could do your paperwork for you."

"All his arrest reports would say the same thing," she said. "'Found bad man, bit bad man, got toy, good boy.'"

"That's poetic," Vic said. "I mean, it's not Russian poetry or anything, but it's a start."

"Of course not," she agreed. "If it were Russian, it'd be full of stuff about vodka."

"And we're back to alcohol abuse," Webb said.

"What do you expect, sir?" Vic asked. "We're Russian and Irish. They build liquor stores on account of people like us."

"On the subject of depression and alcoholism," Webb said, "someone also needs to do family notification."

"I was just saying how much I love doing paperwork, sir," Vic said promptly.

"Damn," Erin muttered.

*   *   *

Given the choice between paperwork and death notifications, it was really a question of a short, extremely unpleasant job versus a long, tediously unpleasant one. But the work had to be done.

According to the receptionist at Ethereal Angels, Sarah Devers came from Athens, Georgia. She had a mother there. Erin had a phone number and an address. She couldn't very well fly down to the deep South on the NYPD's dime, so it would have to be a telephone notification. She picked up her phone and dialed, thinking it would be easier if she got a voicemail. On the other hand, maybe Mrs. Devers would know something that would help crack the case.

On the third ring, a soft, drawling female voice came on the line.

"Hello?"

"Mrs. Devers?" Erin guessed.

"Bless your heart, that makes me sound as old as the hills. Nobody calls me that. Who is this, honey? You're not from around here, I can hear that in your voice."

"Ma'am, my name is Erin O'Reilly. I'm a detective with the New York Police Department." She took a breath. "Are you the mother of Sarah Devers?"

"Of course I am. Oh, dear. My girl hasn't gone and gotten herself in trouble, I hope. I knew when she went to the big city, she'd be in for all sorts of temptations."

"I'm sorry, ma'am. I have some bad news. We found her this morning in a hotel in Manhattan. She died."

"Honey, please speak up. I think I lost the connection for a moment."

Erin sighed inwardly. Sometimes people wouldn't hear something if it was news they didn't want. "Sarah is dead, ma'am."

"Oh sweet Jesus," Mrs. Devers said softly. "My baby girl. My poor baby girl."

"I'm sorry," Erin said again.

"What happened to my little angel?" the woman asked.

"We're working on finding out what happened. At the moment, it appears she may have drowned. Did your daughter have any problems with drugs or alcohol?"

"My Sarah? Absolutely not!" Mrs. Devers sounded more shocked by that suggestion than she had been by the news of Sarah's death. "She wasn't even old enough to drink! And she would never touch drugs. That devil's poison had no hold on her."

"Ma'am, Sarah's seventeen, correct?"

"That's right. Oh dear Lord, my poor girl."

"What was she doing in New York on her own?"

"My Sarah is such a pretty girl," Mrs. Devers said. "Ever since she was very young, all she wanted was to be beautiful.

She always had the loveliest eyes, the most marvelous smile, and that long, silky hair. You know, she won her first beauty pageant. How old do you think she was?"

"How old?" Erin asked, not sure she wanted the answer.

"Seven," Mrs. Devers said proudly. "We tried to give her a normal childhood, within the constraints of the pageant circuit. But she was home-schooled, of course. She won titles in both glitz and natural competitions. My Sarah could charm anyone in the room, male or female."

Erin swallowed and realized she was squeezing the phone too hard. She tried not to think what her dad would say if he heard this woman talk. "And New York?" she heard herself ask.

"Her first adult contract," Mrs. Devers said. "Well, not strictly adult, legally speaking. She got special permission. I had to sign in her name. I leased a small apartment in SoHo. I was planning to move up there with her, but my Sarah wanted to spread her wings. She insisted I stay home. She is so grown-up for her age, so..."

The woman's composure abruptly cracked as the reality of the situation finally came home to her. Erin gave her a few moments to regain her equilibrium.

"I'll put you in touch with someone to help you sort through things," Erin finally said. "In the meantime, we're trying to nail down the events. Do you know anything about Sarah's boyfriend?"

"Boyfriend?" Mrs. Devers echoed, horror breaking through her grief. "My Sarah would never! Not at her age! Keep the boys looking, I always told her, but don't ever let them touch. Touch destroys your mystique. A young lady is to be admired, but from a respectful distance."

Erin's heart sank. From the sound of things, Mrs. Devers had no idea what her daughter had been up to in New York. This conversation wasn't going to be any help.

"I'll give you my phone number," she said. "If you think of anything that might be helpful, please contact me. And talk to the person I'll connect you to. She'll help you with everything."

"My poor girl," Mrs. Devers said again. "All she ever wanted was for people to see how beautiful she was."

*   *   *

After that, it was almost a relief to go back to the paperwork. It was probably a good thing they weren't allowed to throw random people in jail without filing all sorts of official justifications, but that didn't make it less annoying for the arresting officer. She was used to it, however. Every job had something like it, and she reflected it could be worse. She could be doing a job that was nothing but paperwork, in which case she'd probably go clean out of her mind.

At five o' clock, rather than leaving right away, she decided to take a detour to the morgue to see how Levine was coming on the autopsy. She got Rolf and headed downstairs to the cold, sterile basement lair of the Medical Examiner.

Her timing was lousy. Levine had Sarah Devers on the slab, opened up, and was extracting and weighing organs. Erin suppressed a cringe at the sight. She'd never grown accustomed to seeing a human body being disassembled like a used car torn up for spare parts, and she didn't want to.

"Hey, Doc," she said from behind the protection of a hand over her mouth. The smell of blood and chemical preservatives was overpowering. "Do you know what killed her yet?"

"Not yet," Levine said without looking up. "I know some things that didn't kill her."

"That's a start, I guess. What didn't kill her?"

"The lungs have very little water. Cause of death was not drowning."

"So she was dead when she went into the water?"

"She was not breathing when she went into the water," Levine corrected. "It's difficult to say whether she was still alive at that point. A heartbeat may have been present. There was no time for decomposition to occur, nor did the fish show much interest in the body. I know of some preliminary research being done into bone proteins as a marker for how long a body has been submerged, but that method is probably several years away from viability."

"Can you give me a time of death?" Erin asked. "It'd be nice to know how long she was in the water, but I understand if you can't do that."

"Core temperature readings are useless," Levine said.

"Why?" Erin asked.

"The water was kept at tropical temperatures of twenty-seven degrees Celsius and the body had reached equilibrium with the surrounding medium," Levine explained. "Standard human body temperature, of course, is thirty-seven degrees. Bodies cool at approximately one point five degrees per hour in the air, but water can accelerate the process. Regardless, once this body reached the same temperature as the medium, that measurement only shows the victim was deceased seven or more hours before I checked the temperature."

"Better than nothing," Erin said.

"Lividity agrees with the temperature reading," Levine went on. "She was dead at least eight hours before she was found. Rigor mortis was present, but that can be problematic in waterlogged bodies. All I can say with certainty is that the victim has been deceased since at least one o' clock this morning, and not more than twenty-four hours."

"Okay," Erin said. "What else didn't kill her?"

"I found few signs of gross physical trauma. Some of the organs do show signs of light internal damage, but the abdominal flesh shows no significant bruising."

"Meaning what?"

"The victim suffered moderate blunt-force damage to her abdomen, consistent with receiving a beating."

"Can you tell what hit her?"

"My hypothesis is she was struck with bare hands. Most weapons would have left visible contusions."

"And she was only hit in the stomach?"

"These injuries are confined to the abdominal area," Levine said. "The stomach and kidneys, particularly." She picked up one of the kidneys in question and held it out for Erin to examine. Erin tried to look interested and impressed. She was definitely going to eat salad for dinner tonight. Meat was off the menu.

"So someone punched her in the gut?" Erin asked.

"More than once," Levine said.

"And these injuries were inflicted before she died?"

"Definitely. Unfortunately, I can't tell exactly how much time elapsed prior to death."

"Any other injuries?"

"Signs of defensive damage on the right hand." Levine indicated the hand.

"Yeah, we saw the broken fingernails," Erin said. "I guess she put up a fight."

"Not much of a fight," Levine said. "I found no damage to knuckles, no scratches. Curiously, I did find one other thing when I cracked the thoracic cavity."

"What's that?"

"Several ribs have hairline fractures, consistent with repeated hard impacts to the sternum."

"Okay, so she got punched in the chest and stomach," Erin said.

"Repeated impacts to the sternum," Levine repeated in annoyed tones, as if Erin was a particularly slow student. "That bone is very near the surface of the skin. Skin will bruise very easily over the sternum, but the victim's skin does not show bruising consistent with blows from knuckles. These fractures were not caused by blows from a fist. Additionally, I see no sign of bone remodeling. These fractures were inflicted nearly simultaneously with the victim's death."

"Then what..." Erin began. Then she stopped. She felt suddenly foolish. "CPR," she said.

"That is my conclusion," Levine said. "These fractures are consistent with chest compressions, particularly when administered by an amateur."

"You're saying someone tried to save her life?"

Levine nodded.

"That doesn't sound like something a murderer would do," Erin said thoughtfully.

"I don't speculate on psychological profiling," Levine said. "Profiling is a soft and inexact science. Forensic medicine is much more likely to lead to conclusive results."

"Thanks, Doc," Erin said. "Let us know as soon as you have cause of death."

"I'll forward my report as soon as I complete it. And I'll complete it as soon as I'm able to finish working. Without distractions."

That was about as polite a way as Levine had of telling Erin she was getting in the way and it was time to leave. Erin took the cue.

"Thanks," she said again and got away from the morgue and its clinical, chemical-smelling horrors.

*   *   *

Erin had gotten used to stopping by the Barley Corner after work for a drink. Now she lived there. It was a little strange, particularly since she had to assume most of the mob clientele knew exactly where she was living and who she was living with.

Confidence was the way to handle Mob guys. If they smelled fear on you, they'd eat you alive. It was a lot like training an aggressive dog. You didn't want to pick fights, but you had to assert authority. Fortunately, Erin had a lifetime of experience to fall back on as a girl with three brothers, along with twelve years as a cop. She walked into the bar like she owned the place, taking a second to scan the room.

There was Ian Thompson, Carlyle's bodyguard and newly-promoted head of security. He wasn't even thirty years old, but the former Marine Scout Sniper was as tough a man as Erin had ever met, and more reliable than most. He favored her with a slight nod and went right back to watching the room.

Erin recognized a few other faces, all O'Malley guys. A couple of them smiled at her and one waved. It was weird being accepted by mobsters as one of them, but that was the point of her undercover work.

She saw James Corcoran at a booth on one side of the room. He appeared to be chatting up a woman, which wasn't unusual, but the woman appeared to be older and heavier than his usual target. Then Erin recognized the woman and all her confidence dropped right out of her. At that moment, Corky, feeling eyes on him, looked up.

"Ah, there's the very lass," he said cheerfully. "How's the business of coppering, love?"

"Hi, Corky," Erin said. Then, biting the bullet, "Hi, Mom."

Chapter 6

Erin stood in the Barley Corner, watching her two worlds smash into each other. Her thoughts were racing. What did Mary O'Reilly know? Erin had told her dad about Carlyle, but had asked him not to tell her mom about the gangster. But then she'd moved in with Carlyle and she'd hardly been able to keep that a secret from her family. She'd called her mom to tell her the news the day before yesterday. Erin tried to remember exactly what she'd said.

"I'm moving in with a guy, Mom."

"What? Erin? Honey, when? Who is this guy? How long have you known him? Does your father know? But of course he does. He's been so close-mouthed the last few days. Oh my goodness. This is the man who was shot in your apartment? What's his name?"

"One question at a time, Mom. His name's Morton Carlyle. He runs a pub downtown, just a couple blocks from where I've been living."

"A bar owner?"

"Yeah, Mom. I've been going to his place after work a lot, we got to talking, and we found out we've got a lot in common. I helped him out with a couple of things and... you know, one thing led to another."

"How old is he?"

"He just turned fifty."

"Isn't that a little old for you, dear?"

"It's a fourteen-year gap, Mom. It's not the end of the world. He's in good shape, he's healthy. Well, except for getting shot."

"When are you bringing him up to meet us?"

"Mom, he's just getting out of the hospital. This isn't a good time."

"Oh, of course not. How long have you been seeing him?"

"Since around New Year."

"Erin!"

"Sorry, Mom. It's just that work's been crazy, and I've got a lot going on in my life, and I thought Dad might not approve. It's complicated."

Complicated, Erin thought ruefully. That word didn't even begin to cover it. "I didn't know you were coming down," she said. "You should've called. You know I keep unusual hours. You might've been waiting all night."

"Not to worry, love," Corky said brightly. "I'd have made sure to keep her entertained. After all, you're practically family. No kin of yours will be wanting for anything I can provide."

"I came down to the city to do some shopping," Mary said. "I'll be staying with Junior and Shelley tonight. What time is it?"

"About five-thirty," Erin said.

"Oh, my!" her mother said. "The time does fly. I should let Shelley know if I won't be there for supper. I've been talking to this nice gentleman for over an hour. He tells the most charming stories from the old country."

Erin gave Corky a hard, penetrating look. It bounced right off him.

"Did Dad come with you?" she asked.

"No, he went out on a fishing trip with a couple of his friends. One of them just bought a new boat and had to show it off. They're probably drinking beer and eating hot dogs on the lake about now. I wasn't invited." She smiled. "So here I am. Now where's this gentleman friend Mr. Corcoran's been telling me so much about?"

"It's Corky to my friends, Mary," Corky said, patting her hand. "I've told you that."

"Where is he?" Erin asked Corky.

"Haven't an earthly, love. I've not seen him this afternoon. I'm thinking he's probably resting in bed, as a lad does when he's had a few extra holes punched in him."

"I'd better check on him," Erin said. "And see if he's up for hosting."

"Nonsense, dear," Mary said briskly, getting to her feet. "I raised three boys and a girl all the way to adulthood. I cared for all four of you through the chicken pox. Then there was your broken arm, not to mention Michael's whooping cough and Junior's bout with croup. If your man needs care, I'm quite capable of providing it. I'll be happy to prepare whatever he's allowed to eat."

"Mom," Erin said gently, "he owns a bar and restaurant. There's a kitchen right here."

"Oh." Mary deflated slightly. Feeding people was the best way she knew to take care of them.

There was no point in drawing it out. Better to get it over with. Erin took a deep breath.

"But let's go see him. Just remember, he's barely out of the hospital."

Mary beamed. She took a bag out from under the table and started after her daughter. "It was very nice meeting you, Corky," she said.

"Likewise, Mary," he said. "I hope to be seeing much more of you in the future." Then he winked and bent in to give her a quick kiss on the cheek.

Mary gasped in surprise, but didn't seem entirely displeased. "It's been a long time since a strange man tried to kiss me in a bar," she said.

"And it'll be a long time before he tries it again," Erin said. "If he knows what's good for him." She steered her mother away from the grinning Irishman.

Halfway across the room, Ian stepped away from the wall. Somehow managing not to be impolite, he got between Mary and the door. His eyes were on her bag.

"Ian, it's okay," Erin said, recognizing the sudden tension in his posture. "This is my mom, Mary. Mom, this is Ian Thompson. He's the... bouncer."

"Ma'am," Ian said politely. "Can I ask what's in the bag?"

"It's a Bundt cake," Mary said. "Homemade. Chocolate with cream cheese frosting." She glanced at Erin. "Is something wrong?"

"Forget about it," Erin told Ian. Then she turned to her mother. "Ian was in Iraq and Afghanistan. He dealt with IEDs and roadside bombs, so he doesn't like strange packages. He didn't mean anything."

"No disrespect, ma'am," Ian said.

"Thank you for your service, young man," Mary said.

"My pleasure, ma'am."

"Ian saved my life a week ago," Erin said. "Carlyle's, too."

"Oh!" Mary exclaimed. Then, to Ian's utter consternation, she set the cake bag on the floor and put her arms around him in a sudden, spontaneous, and enveloping embrace.

Ian Thompson was a man of action, a combat veteran Carlyle had once called the most dangerous man in New York City. But he'd never faced an opponent like Mary. He stiffened, and Erin saw a whole series of emotions dance across his normally-stoic face, but he carefully put one arm around the O'Reilly matriarch and awkwardly returned the hug.

"Just doing my job, ma'am," he said.

"Nonsense," Mary said. "I'm glad you were there to look after my little girl."

"She looks after herself just fine, ma'am. Now please, excuse me. I'm working." Ian disengaged himself and returned to his place by the wall.

"What a fine young man," Mary said. "Quiet, but so polite. It's rare these days."

"He's a good guy," Erin said, retrieving the cake before someone could kick it across the room.

"So tell me about Morton," Mary said as Erin got out her key.

"First off, I don't call him Morton," Erin said. "Nobody calls him that."

"What do you call him, dear?"

"Just Carlyle. His friends call him Cars, but I don't like the nickname."

"Why do they call him that? Does he like to drive?"

Erin pretended she hadn't heard the question. The nickname came from Carlyle's IRA days, when he'd built car bombs for the paramilitary group. Her mom didn't need to hear that. She got the door open and ushered Mary and Rolf in, making sure the door locked behind the three of them.

"I'm home!" Erin called quietly, hoping not to wake Carlyle if he was asleep.

"Grand," his voice came from the living room. "And who's with you?"

"My mom came down for a visit," she said. "Are you decent?"

"If you'll give me half a moment."

The O'Reillys paused at the top of the stairs. After a minute or so, Carlyle spoke again.

"Come in, please."

Erin had expected to find him in a bathrobe, or maybe pajamas. But that wasn't Carlyle. He'd apparently needed the pause in order to tie his necktie and throw on his suit coat. When Erin and her mother entered the living room, Carlyle looked as sharp and put-together as ever. He was standing, as he always did when a woman entered the room.

"You didn't need to put on the tie," Erin said.

"If I'm making a first impression, I'd best make it a grand one," he said. "Mrs. O'Reilly, I presume?"

"It's Mary, dear," Erin's mom said, offering her hand. Carlyle took it, bent over it, and kissed it.

"Aren't you the gentleman," Mary said. "Erin tells me you don't like to be called by your given name. What should I call you?"

"Carlyle will do," he said. "I'm charmed to meet you. I'm only sorry I'd no greater warning you were coming. I'd have taken some extra pains on your behalf."

"Speaking of pain, sit down," Erin said. "You shouldn't be walking around more than you need to." She'd seen the lines of strain on his face, though he did a good job hiding them.

"Since you ask," he said, sinking onto the couch. "You'll be staying for supper, surely."

"I don't want to put you to any trouble," Mary said.

"It's no trouble, truly," he said. "I'll just have the kitchen send something up. Anything off the menu, you've only to ask."

"They make a great Irish stew," Erin said.

"And steak and kidney pie," Carlyle added.

Erin's stomach lurched, remembering the morgue. "But I'm just having a salad tonight."

"You're too thin already, dear," Mary said. "If you want to carry a healthy baby, those hips could use a little more meat on them."

Erin choked. Carlyle's eyes widened and he shot Erin a quick look.

"Mom!" Erin gasped. "It's a little early for that!"

"Never too early," Mary said pleasantly. "I take it you're a good Catholic, Mr. Carlyle?"

"I missed Mass this past weekend," he said. "On account of my injury. But it's the first one I've missed in quite a few years."

"That's good," Mary said. Erin pictured her mom checking an item off her internal checklist. "Erin hasn't been quite so regular in her attendance, I'm afraid. She tells me you own the establishment downstairs?"

"It's my name on the title, aye," he said. What he didn't add was that Evan O'Malley's money had put his name there.

"Erin hasn't told me very much about you," she went on. "From your accent, and from talking with your friend downstairs, I understand you were born in Ireland?"

"Belfast," he confirmed.

"And do you have any family on this side of the Atlantic?"

"It's just me."

"Then it's settled," Mary said. "Erin will be bringing you to our next family get-together."

"I'm grateful for the invitation," he said. "But that's Erin's decision, I'm thinking."

"Nonsense. We'll be glad to have you. You can meet the rest of the family. Though..." Mary paused and furrowed her brow. "You look a little familiar, for some reason. I feel like I've seen you before."

"It's possible. Erin tells me she grew up in Queens. I lived there when I first came over, almost twenty years ago. Though if you remember a chance meeting from so far back, you've a right keen mind."

"That's true," Mary said. "We did live in Queens. Sean and I moved upstate when he retired. What are your views on marriage, Mr. Carlyle?"

"Mom!" Erin exclaimed.

"It's all right, darling," Carlyle said with a gentle smile. "Your mum's only looking out for you. If I'd a daughter, I'd be at least as hard on any lad she brought round. I'm only lucky your da's not here. He'd be even harder on me, I'm thinking."

Carlyle had dodged the question with his usual skill. Erin wondered whether Mary would remember the circumstances later. Erin knew that was the truth. She also suspected her mother had remembered the time a much younger Carlyle had come by their house, back when she was a teenager, and had given her dad the information on his partner proving the other cop had been dirty. That had saved Sean O'Reilly's career, but at a cost two generations of O'Reillys were still calculating.

"You don't have to answer that question about marriage," she said.

"It's all right," he repeated. "I've been wedded once before, Mary. Just for three years, but they were the finest years I've known. Before I met your daughter, of course."

"Divorced?" Mary asked with a twist in the corner of her mouth. She didn't approve of divorce.

"She died," Carlyle replied.

"Oh! I'm so terribly sorry!" Mary was instantly contrite. "You must think I'm horrible, bringing that up." She wanted to give him a hug, Erin saw it in her face, but she remembered his injury at the last moment and settled for putting a hand on his arm.

"Thank you for your concern," he said. "Losing Rosie was a terrible blow. But we all have troubles in this life, and that was a long time ago."

"And what do you think about children?" Mary asked, recovering.

Erin squirmed. She didn't like having her mother pry into her boyfriend's life like this. She already felt like too many people were looking in at them. The last thing she needed was for her family to be judging her while she was trying to keep up appearances for the Mob.

"I'm fond of children," Carlyle said evenly.

"And of having your own?" Mary pressed on.

"I've yet to be so blessed."

"I've been starting to worry about Erin," Mary confided, patting him on the knee. "She's working all the time, with no chance for any sort of normal social life. And you know, I sometimes think her dog stands in place of a baby for her."

Erin and Rolf exchanged a look. "He's my partner, Mom," Erin said. "He's no baby. He just bit a guy who jumped me this afternoon."

"No harm done to you or Rolf, I trust," Carlyle said.

"It wasn't a big deal," she said. "But I wouldn't take a baby along on a felony arrest."

Rolf sat beside Erin looking proud, and maybe just a little bit smug.

*　*　*

Dinner went well. Carlyle was polite, pleasant, and charming. Mary backed off a little on the questioning, though she did ask about Ian.

"Erin tells me your bouncer saved both your lives," she said.

"Aye," he said. "Though it was a close shave for me. Ian's a good lad."

"What was he doing at Erin's apartment?"

"In addition to his other duties, he's my driver."

"You don't drive?"

"I've an unfortunate tendency to drift toward the left side of the road," he laughed. "I'm told Americans prefer to drive on the right."

"Tell me a little about Ian. How do you know him?"

"He was something of a wild lad in his youth," Carlyle said. "His mum was gone and his da wasn't doing any particular good for him. I took him under my wing while he finished his primary schooling. When he came out of the Marines, he asked if I'd a job for him. He's been working for me ever since."

Mary nodded. "That's very kind of you, looking after the poor boy. I'm surprised no eligible woman has snapped you up before now."

"A lass like Erin's one in a million," he said. "And well worth waiting a few years to find."

"Careful, Mom," Erin said. "They say Carlyle can talk his way out of anything."

"I can imagine," she said. "I really don't understand why you haven't told me about him before."

"What do you think of the food?" Erin asked. It was a shaky, obvious change of subject, but she really didn't want to talk about their history more than she had to.

"It's delicious. The stew is just like my mother used to make. It was a recipe that came from the old country."

"As is this," Carlyle said. "And not to worry, Mary. I'm certain we'll be seeing more of one another in the future. You don't know me yet, but you will, I've no doubt."

They finished the meal. Erin got out a bottle of red wine from Carlyle's private stock and they sat up talking into the evening. Erin was constantly aware of Mary's scrutiny, but Carlyle was masterful at deflecting awkward questions. When her mother finally got up to leave, Erin felt the visit had been a success.

"I'll be sure to tell Sean all about you," Mary said. "You seem to be taking good care of my daughter, Mr. Carlyle."

"I think it's rather more a question of her taking care of me at present," he said with a smile. "But we'll manage. It's been a great pleasure meeting you, Mary O'Reilly. You've raised a fine lass and you've every right to be proud of her."

"Thank you," she said. "Sean thinks the world of her too, though he doesn't always say so. When Junior was born, he thought he'd follow him into the police, but little Sean never took to it. Erin was always the tough one of the four."

"Still am," Erin said.

"My husband keeps an eye on her," Mary confided. "Through his old friends in the Department."

"Yeah, I know," Erin said, rolling her eyes. "I can feel them looking over my shoulder."

"It's for your own good, dear."

"I know. It's been great having you here, Mom. Now you can stop worrying about me."

"We'll see about that. Good night, dear."

* * *

"Sorry for springing that on you," Erin said. She'd walked her mom to the front door and returned to the apartment, so she and Carlyle were now alone. "I swear, I didn't know she was coming."

"As far as being surprised by alarming people goes, darling, this scarcely registers," Carlyle said with a smile. "Your mum's a fine lass."

"I don't think anyone's called her a lass in years. Except maybe Corky. Oh God, she was talking to Corky. For an hour. Unsupervised."

"Not to worry, darling. She's a mite old for him."

"Ugh. That wasn't what I was worried about. But I am now. Thanks for that. He could've told her things."

"Haven't you learned? Corky's a master of the art of talking while saying nothing at all."

Erin laughed. "You're right about that. I just don't think we need this extra trouble right now."

Carlyle was still smiling, but his eyes grew more serious. "Erin, building the case for your lads is going to take time. It'll be months before all's ready, as you well know. Did you really think your family would just sit by and wait? You're a close-knit clan. I'm certain I'll be seeing all the rest of them before long. You're not ashamed of me, are you?"

"Well... no," she said. "But it's complicated. If I could just tell them you were helping me infiltrate the Mob, they'd think you were a hero. But we can't say that, so I don't want to talk about what it looks like you're doing. Because what it looks like..."

"Is that I'm living a sordid life of crime?"

"Yeah, pretty much."

"But you fell in love with me before I started cooperating with the coppers," he reminded her.

"That's different."

"How?"

"It just is!" She scowled at him. "You're yanking me around."

"Perhaps a little. If we can't find the funny side of this, it's going to be a grim year."

"You think it'll take a whole year?"

He shrugged. "That's up to your lads, particularly when it comes to what they're prepared to accept. If all they're wanting is to throw a few lads behind bars for a couple of years, we can get that done any time we like. We could do that tomorrow. The only downside is, I'd be dead inside a week, and possibly you along with me. But if we're truly wanting a clean sweep, your district attorney will be needing financial records, taped conversations, bank accounts, the whole works."

"But you've got the financial records," she said.

He shook his head. "Not nearly all of them. The only things I've got are the books for the Barley Corner and a few other businesses, all doctored to look legitimate. What you're needing is Evan's main ledger."

"Which you can get your hands on?"

He shook his head again. "Nay, I don't even know where he keeps it. Without that, we've no way of knowing how far his reach goes. I can tell your lads most of the businesses Evan's invested in, but it'll be bloody hard to prove. And then we've got to tie all the major players to as many crimes as possible. It'll be a bookkeeping nightmare. Not to mention the risks you and I will be taking whenever we wire up for a conversation."

"Yeah, I remember," Erin said sourly. "The last O'Malley meeting I went to, I wasn't wearing a wire and Mickey still almost killed me."

"Speaking of which," he said. "You mentioned you were in a bit of a scrap today?"

"Oh, that. It was nothing. Just a dumbass perp who tried to shove past me. I took him down and he hadn't had enough yet, so Rolf finished the job. I wasn't even scratched."

"Is he the lad you're looking for?"

"I think so. But there's still some loose ends to tie up."

"I hope it'll keep until tomorrow. I'd rather looked forward to your company tonight."

"Well, here I am." She spread her hands wide. "You've got your girlfriend living with you now. How do you like it?"

"I'd have liked to carry you over the threshold," he said. "But doctor's orders, I fear. The same for properly christening our joint residence. My muscles aren't quite up for what we'd both be wanting, sad to say."

"That's all right. It gives us something to look forward to." She slid in close to him on the sofa and kissed him. "At least I can do this. What harm can a kiss do?"

"I seem to recall it ending poorly for our Lord and savior in Gethsemane," he said, smiling. "But I'll take my chances." He slid his hand around the back of her neck and drew her in close.

Chapter 7

Webb was already in the Major Crimes office when Erin arrived the next morning. Fortified by coffee, he was typing away at his computer.

"Let me guess, sir," Erin said. "Levine stayed overnight to finish the bloodwork."

"It's like you know her," Webb said. "The results should be on your computer."

"Homicide?" she guessed, sliding into her chair and flipping on her monitor. Rolf, recognizing the signs of impending boredom, settled onto his belly with a sigh. He wriggled around into a comfortable position on his blanket next to Erin's desk.

"Sort of."

"Sort of?" she echoed. Those were not typical words for Levine to attach to a report.

"We can charge it as a homicide," he said.

"Then what's the problem?"

"Cause of death was apparently a drug overdose."

"Oh." Erin had the report up on her screen now. She quickly skimmed it, trying to parse Levine's dry medical jargon. "What drug?"

"Rohypnol, probably exacerbated by alcohol."

"Someone roofied her?"

"Yeah." Webb sighed. "It used to be, you only had to worry about that in seedy bars. Now we've got a charity dinner at an upscale hotel."

"Couldn't have happened at dinner, sir," she said. "If Devers had enough Rohypnol to kill her, there's no way she could've gone up to Stone's room and talked afterward. She wouldn't have been conscious."

"Unless Stone is lying," Webb said. "But we should be able to tell if she was drugged at dinner by looking at the security tape again. If she left the room under her own power, she wasn't under the influence yet. That stuff hits you within half an hour and it hits hard."

"Nobody takes Rohypnol recreationally," Erin said. "If she had it in her system, somebody drugged her, probably with the intention to rape her."

"I agree," Webb said.

"That absolutely makes this a homicide, whether they meant to kill her or not."

"I agree," he repeated. "And we'll treat it as such. But we need to consider the other results of the autopsy."

Erin took a moment to look over the report some more. "No signs of sexual assault," she said. "That doesn't mean anything, sir. If she went down hard from the drugs, it just means her assailant didn't like the idea of getting cozy with a corpse."

"Understandable," Webb said. "There's also the cracked ribs."

"Either the person who drugged her tried to keep her alive, or some Good Samaritan did," Erin said.

"Not a very good one in my opinion," Webb said. "Given that the CPR was probably the last thing that happened before she got dumped in the fish tank. A real Samaritan would've called 911 instead of tossing her in the water."

"So either the person trying to save her was working with the person who drugged her, or they're the same person," Erin said.

"I'm guessing there's only one subject," Webb said. "When in doubt, go with the simple option."

"Maybe," she said. "But I'm thinking about the broken fingernails."

"What about them?"

"Devers put up a struggle. She had to be conscious for that. And there's another thing."

"What?"

"The power outage."

"Right," Webb said. "Convenient, wasn't it? The power goes out just when we need it to see the body getting moved? You think there's any chance that's a coincidence?"

"Sir, if I believed in playing those odds, I'd go buy a lottery ticket right now."

"I'd go halves with you," he said. "Forget about my pension. I think we need to look into the hotel custodial staff. You've got the list of workers who were on the night shift?"

"Yeah."

"Start checking them for criminal records, especially sex offenses."

"The hotel wouldn't have hired a registered sex offender."

"Background checks miss things. We won't know until we look. To hell with Sherlock Holmes. Fancy logic doesn't solve as many cases as just putting your nose to the grindstone."

"I'll start grinding, sir. But what about Schilling?"

"What about him?" Webb smiled grimly. "He's not going anywhere."

*   *   *

Vic arrived a few minutes later and was promptly put to work on the same task Erin was doing. Background checks weren't difficult, but they took time. The detectives had to double-check residency history and neighboring states' records to make sure nobody had done a crime in, say, New Jersey before moving to New York. They had to check for name changes and juvenile records. And they looked at charges that hadn't stuck. An employer wouldn't know about a case that had been thrown out, or that had led to an acquittal, but Erin and Vic were looking for possible patterns of behavior. Just because the law didn't say a guy was guilty didn't mean he hadn't done it. To a police officer's eye, that could just mean the perp had gotten away with it.

"I got nothing but misdemeanor crap," Vic said after a couple of hours. "Some disorderly conduct, a couple drunk and disorderly, one public intoxication, and a few half-ass reefer busts. You?"

"I looked over Mr. Stone, the guy who invited her up for drinks, as long as I was doing checks. He's clean. No charges at all, here or in Massachusetts," Erin said. "I've did find one guy that's interesting, though. An electrician. He's been arrested a few times, but no charges ever stuck."

"What'd we grab him for?" Vic asked, rolling his chair toward her desk.

"A couple bar fights and an assault."

"How come he didn't do any time?"

Erin looked over the arrest reports. "The brawls didn't result in anyone pressing charges. Looks like they were just a bunch of drunken idiots smacking each other around."

"Sounds like my typical Friday nights," Vic said.

"The only one that was serious, someone went to the hospital. The problem is, it was our guy who got hospitalized. The complainant was a girl who said she saw him slip something in her drink while he was chatting her up."

"Ooh, I like that," Vic said. "That's solid."

"I don't know." Erin frowned at her computer screen. "The girl teaches Krav Maga at a martial arts club in Brooklyn. She took the glass he'd spiked and broke it in his face."

"Ouch." Vic winced.

"Then she kicked him in the crotch and dislocated his shoulder," Erin continued. "She didn't even have a bruise, and she'd lost the evidence of the drug when she smashed the glass, so the DA didn't have a case."

"How come he didn't press assault charges on her?" Vic asked.

"Take a look," she said, pointing to her computer. There, side by side, were pictures of the young woman and her alleged assailant. The guy was a hulking brute of a man, matching Vic's six-foot-three frame and sporting a bushy beard. He was also showing an obviously broken nose, a swollen eye, and numerous facial lacerations. The girl was listed as five-foot-two and a hundred and ten pounds.

"Jesus," Vic said. "He's like three of her."

"I guess he didn't want to shrink what was left of his manhood by publicly declaring he got his ass handed to him by a tiny woman," Erin said.

"She looks kinda like our victim," Vic commented.

"Yeah," Erin said. "Same facial shape, a little shorter but a similar build. But I guess Sarah Devers didn't know kung fu."

"Krav Maga," Vic corrected. "I took a class once from this guy, ex-Israeli special forces. I'm not surprised this girl wrecked him. He's just lucky she didn't go for the eyes. So where's this electrician now? Who is he?"

"His name's Lloyd Polk," she said. "He's still living in Brooklyn. Rough commute. The InterContinental has him working nights."

"What do you bet he's got access to the fusebox?"

"A week's pay says he does." Erin raised her voice and called across the room. "Sir?"

"What is it?" Webb replied. He'd been examining the autopsy report and hadn't been paying attention to their conversation.

"Got an electrician with a history of violence, access to the hotel power grid, and a charge last year that he tried to slip a woman a mickey."

"Go bring him in," Webb said.

"We've already got a guy in lockup for this," Erin reminded him.

"We've got space," he replied. "No one's been charged yet. Go talk to this guy, find out what he's got to say. Maybe they're in it together."

"I'll go with her," Vic volunteered.

"You want to ride with O'Reilly?" Webb asked, surprised. Vic and Erin had been on rocky personal ground ever since he'd learned about her and Carlyle. They were working together okay, but it wouldn't be true to say they were completely happy with each other.

"No, sir," Vic said cheerfully. "I'm just hoping this mope wants to resist arrest. I bet he'd love to see what a guy my size can do with Krav Maga. You can drive, Erin."

* * *

In Erin's Charger, on the way down to Brooklyn, Vic sat in the passenger seat. Rolf was in his compartment. Both of them were obviously hoping for action.

Erin wasn't sure. She didn't mind throwing down with a goon, particularly when the mope liked taking advantage of women. But she still thought Schilling was the more likely perp, and they didn't have a single bit of evidence tying Polk to Devers's death. All they had was an unproven allegation by someone who'd beaten the crap out of the guy. Still, everyone was judged by their past actions, so they had to at least talk to him. She just hoped Vic wasn't too eager to beat him down.

"Hey, Vic?" she asked after a few minutes.

"Yeah?"

"I can only say I'm sorry so many times." She had to be careful what she said here. Her car might very well be bugged by Internal Affairs.

"I don't hate you," he sighed. "I hate that smooth jerk you're hanging out with, but I don't hate you. He's gonna hurt you, Erin. Or the people you love. He's not worth it."

"How would you know if he's worth it?" she shot back.

"Hey, look, I've had good sex, okay?"

Erin grimaced. "A little too much information, Vic, but okay, I believe you."

"And no sex is good enough to go through that much trouble."

"It's not about the sex, Vic."

"So now you're not screwing him?"

"Of course not. He just got out of the hospital. I don't want to kill him."

"That's a good point," Vic said. He gave her a considering look. "You really think you'd kill him? I mean, I know he's old and all, but damn, girl. A lot of people talk about having a killer body, but you really take it to the next level."

"Are you joking, Vic? I can't always tell."

"I like to keep you guessing."

Erin gave it a few moments, just long enough for him to think she'd dropped the subject.

Then she said, "I bet Piekarski could kill you."

Vic snorted a startled laugh. "You got no idea."

"How's things going with her?" Erin asked. Zofia Piekarski was a plainclothes cop with the Street Narcotics Enforcement Unit, a petite blonde who had a casual relationship with Vic.

"Fine. She thinks I'd make a good SNEU cop."

"You would. They could use you for all the black-market steroid buy-and-busts. You look like you juice."

"I'll take that as a compliment."

"You know what happens when you use steroids?"

"I'm not sure this is a compliment anymore."

"Your balls shrink like little raisins."

"Good thing mine were so big to begin with," he said.

*   *   *

Lloyd Polk's apartment was an old brick building on 7th Street in Gowanus. It was mid-morning on a workday, so the place was pretty much deserted. Erin parked across the street and unloaded Rolf.

"Brooklyn," Vic said, taking a deep breath. "I love this place."

"Feels like coming home?" Erin guessed. Vic had grown up in Brighton Beach in the Russian immigrant neighborhood called Little Odessa.

"Nope. It reminds me why I left. Every time I come back to Long Island, I remember how much worse life can get and I feel better about myself." He grinned savagely. "Speaking of which, let's see how bad we can make this dirtbag's life."

They climbed a non-handicap-accessible concrete staircase to the door and buzzed the super. They showed their shields to the man, who let them in while insisting he didn't want any trouble.

"No drugs here, man," he kept saying to Vic. "My people, they're clean. We got none of that stuff here. No drugs."

"We're not here about drugs," Erin said. "We want Lloyd Polk. Our records say he lives here."

"Polk? Yeah, he's up in 208," the super said. "But he doesn't do drugs. He works downtown, a legitimate job."

"I said this isn't about drugs," she said.

"Some of these guys, they're out on the street corners, they're selling drugs, but I don't want none of that around me," he insisted.

Erin started to say something else and met Vic's look. He rolled his eyes and shook his head. She shrugged, shut up, and went upstairs to apartment 208.

"What do you bet the super's dealing drugs?" he said under his breath.

"No bet," Erin said. "Maybe you better drop a tip to your girlfriend and have SNEU sniff around a little."

"Good idea. Looks like we're here." Vic pounded on the door with his big, heavy fist. "Hey! Open up! This is the NYPD! We want to talk to you!"

"Subtle, Vic," Erin said. "Real subtle."

"If you wanted subtle, you should've left me in the car," he said. Then he banged on the door again. "Come on! We know you're in there! You want me to break this door down?"

"Okay, okay," came a muffled, groggy voice. "I'm comin.'"

Erin dropped back half a step and rested her hand near the butt of her pistol, just in case. You never knew what would happen when a suspect opened a door.

The lock clicked and the door swung open about two inches, revealing the chain lock and a sliver of bearded, suspicious face.

"Lloyd Polk?" Vic asked.

"Yeah," the guy said. "How do I know you're the cops?"

Vic held up his gold shield.

"You coulda got that out of a cereal box," Polk said.

"I'm a bacon and eggs guy," Vic replied, deadpan.

"Whaddaya want?"

"Want to talk to you, ask you some questions."

"What about?"

"May we come in, sir?" Erin asked.

Polk's gaze shifted to her. He liked what he saw. His eyes traveled up and down her, undressing her with his eyes. "Sure," he said. "Just a sec."

He disengaged the chain lock and opened the door. Vic, Erin, and Rolf stepped into what was obviously a bachelor apartment. The smells alone would have tipped Erin off. She caught a whiff of sweat, cigarette smoke, and unwashed dishes. The curtains were heavy blackout jobs, which made sense given his schedule.

Lloyd Polk looked like he belonged in the place. He was an enormous mound of fat and hair, his beard covering the top few inches of a dirty white T-shirt. His eyes looked too small for his face, beady and unpleasant. They reminded Erin of rodent eyes.

"You woke me up," Polk said. "I work nights."

"We know," Erin said. "We need to talk to you about what happened the night before last."

"Whaddaya mean, what happened? I was at work."

"At the InterContinental," Vic said.

"Yeah. So?"

"Tell us about Crystal Winters," Erin said.

"Crystal what?" Polk asked. "Is that a drink, or a song, or what?"

"Stop playing dumb," Vic snapped. "Focus. Crystal Winters. Do you know her or not?"

"Know who?" Polk asked.

"Not sure he's playing," Erin said quietly.

"Okay, listen up, Einstein," Vic growled. "We're gonna show you a picture and you're gonna tell us what you know about her. You think you can handle that?"

Polk shrugged. "You gonna tell me what's goin' on?"

Erin produced a crime scene photo. It was a shot the CSU guys had taken right before Hank and Ernie had retrieved the body. Sarah Devers floated in the aquarium, eyes wide and staring, pale porcelain skin standing out against the dark water. The effect was startling and eerie.

"What is this?" Polk demanded.

"Do you recognize this girl?" Erin asked.

"Uh, yeah. I think so."

"Where did you see her?"

"At the hotel."

"When?"

"Two nights ago. Comin' outta the ballroom with some rich sugar daddy on her arm."

"She looked good, didn't she?" Erin asked.

Polk licked his lips and leered at her. "Hell yeah, she did. I'd tap that ass any day of the week."

Erin suppressed a shudder of disgust. "What were you doing outside the ballroom?"

"We had a wiring problem in one of the lights over the stairs, flaky connection. It was makin' the bulb flicker. I was up on a ladder, puttin' it back together."

"Did you see where she went?"

"Yeah, she got in the elevator with the rich prick. Probably so he could take her upstairs and pop some Viagra, get it on. He was paying for it. Had to be, only way a babe like that would get with that guy."

"Did you see her leave the hotel?" Erin asked.

"Nah. Guess he paid for the whole night." Polk made an expressive thrusting motion with his hand while looking right in Erin's eyes. She didn't give him the pleasure of a reaction.

"You got any roofies around here?" Vic asked abruptly, glancing around the apartment.

"Huh?" Polk looked confused for a second, then alarmed. "No! Of course not!"

"You sure about that?" Vic asked.

"Look, if this is about that bitch in that bar, she lied about it. I'm the one who got hurt! You oughta be arresting her!"

"Yeah, she sure looked dangerous," Vic said with a gleam in his eye. "I bet you hardly knew what hit you."

"She was a lot stronger than she looked," Polk said sullenly. "You shoulda seen the way she moved."

"Sounds to me like you had it coming," Vic said. "Trying to drug a girl just so you could get off. Real big man."

"Screw you! They didn't prove nothing!"

"So you've never slipped a girl a mickey?" Erin asked. "Or gotten one drunk on purpose?"

Polk glared at her. "I sure as shit didn't drug that Crystal what's-her-name. I'm telling you, I only saw her for a couple seconds!"

"Look at the picture again," Erin said. "Jog your memory."

He glanced at it. Then he paused. "Wait a second. She's not, like, swimming, is she?"

"No," Erin said grimly. "She's not."

Polk stepped back, holding out his hands. "Whoa, whoa, whoa. Wait just a minute. You sayin' this bitch is dead? And you're thinkin' it was me?"

"Maybe you're not so dumb after all," Vic said. "You handle the hotel's electrical systems. So you've got keys to the fuse-box and you know how to use it."

"Well, yeah. What's that got to do with anything?"

"So you turned off the power to the third floor for half an hour. Why?"

"I didn't!"

"Then who did?"

"I don't know! I fixed it when they called me, that's all I know!"

Vic followed Polk as the man backed across the room. "Not good enough, asshole. You tell me what I want to know, or I'm taking you downtown."

"I'm not goin' down for this!" Polk shouted. "You just want someone to pin it on and you saw that bitch's story! Get away from me!"

"That's it," Vic said. "Turn around and put your hands on the wall."

"You can't do this!" Polk protested. "I got rights!"

"Yeah, you do. You've got the right to remain silent. You've got the right to an attorney, and believe me, you're gonna need one. If you can't afford one, which it looks like you can't, you've got the right to some twenty-five-year-old public defender just out of law school who's guaranteed to screw up your case. So if you're smart, you'll plead out and take a deal. Do you understand these rights?"

Erin was standing back to cover Vic, though she figured he had the situation under control. But then she saw the sudden tenseness in Polk's shoulders. "Watch it!" she started to shout, but things were already happening.

Polk had started to obey Vic's instructions. But then, energized by fear and sheer desperation, he spun around, sending an elbow straight into Vic's head. Vic was a good close-quarters fighter, fast, strong, and experienced, but all it took was one unlucky hit to ruin any fist-fighter's day. Polk's elbow caught him square on the temple and sent him reeling, momentarily stunned.

"Rolf! *Fass!*" Erin shouted for the second time in as many days. She lunged beside her dog.

Polk didn't have martial-arts training. What he had was a lot of practice in drunken bar brawls. He stepped behind Vic's stumbling body, using him as a shield. Rolf's teeth clicked shut less than an inch from his arm. The Shepherd's momentum carried him past the guy to crash into the wall. The K-9 went off his feet for a second, but was twisting and scrambling to get up and back in the fight before he hit the ground.

Erin tried to hook a foot behind Polk's leg. She made contact, but he was just too big and heavy to pull down that way. The goon stiff-armed her in the chest, forcing her back a step.

Vic swung a wild fist and hit Polk a looping right hook to the cheek. Polk responded with a vicious head-butt. Erin heard a wet crunch, like someone biting down on a mouthful of milk-soaked cornflakes. Vic's knees buckled.

Erin saw Polk's hand scrabbling at Vic's waist. *Shit, he's going for Vic's gun!* The thought passed through her head much faster than speech. Things had gotten way out of hand. She snatched out her own Glock and thought, *He's a big guy. Two in the chest, one in the head to make sure he goes down.* She saw Polk's hand yank Vic's pistol out of its holster.

"Drop it!" Erin shouted, bringing her gun in line and sliding her finger inside the trigger guard.

Polk howled in surprise and pain. He dropped the gun. The Sig-Sauer automatic skidded across the floor, fetching up against the baseboard at the foot of the wall.

Rolf was behind Polk. In direct disobedience to his training, he'd seized on the most readily available part of his opponent. He was supposed to go for the weapon arm, but that had been out of reach, so he'd improvised by sinking his teeth into Polk's meaty buttocks. Now he hung on, front paws suspended in midair, his whole weight dangling from his teeth.

Erin almost felt sorry for the guy. Still howling, Polk sank to his knees. That took some of the dog's weight off his lacerated ass, but it didn't look like it was helping much.

Erin stepped in and snapped a handcuff on his right wrist. She twisted the arm around behind him a little harder than strictly necessary and grabbed his other arm. Only once Polk was cuffed did she give Rolf his "release" command.

"Rolf! *Pust!*"

The Shepherd immediately opened his jaws and danced back, tail wagging, tongue hanging out, an unmistakable grin on his face. Polk gave a whimper.

Vic got up. One hand was clamped to his face. Blood was running through his fingers. "Son of a bitch," he said in a wet, muffled voice. "He broke my damn nose."

"It's been broken before," Erin said. "Might make you prettier this time. You need a doc?"

"No, I'm good." He glared at Polk. "Or I will be, once we take this piece of shit in."

"You said you wanted to be involved," she reminded him. "What the hell were you thinking?"

"What do you mean?"

"You picked a fight," she hissed. "And then you got your ass kicked."

"He hit me!" Vic protested.

She shook her head. Both of them knew the truth, which was that Vic had been deliberately belligerent. He'd been looking for a fight. Worse, he'd underestimated Polk, probably because Polk had been taken down by a tiny woman. She wanted to hammer the point home, but what was the point? Either he got it or he didn't. Making him mad at her wouldn't help. Besides, just like parents didn't fight in front of the kids, cops shouldn't fight in front of suspects.

She hauled Polk to his feet. "Come on. You can walk, you're fine."

"Crazy dog bit my ass off!" Polk protested.

"And you assaulted a police officer," Erin said. "You're just lucky Rolf got to you before I did. I would've blown your damn stupid head off. What the hell's the matter with you?"

"I didn't do nothing! This is a setup!"

"Yeah, you're a real victim," Vic muttered. "Before we take him in, I'm gonna raid the freezer, get some ice or something."

Chapter 8

"This is going to be good, I can already tell," Webb said.

Vic scowled and held a fast-thawing bag of frozen peas against his face.

"He was uncooperative," Erin said, cocking her head in the direction of the interrogation room, where Lloyd Polk was now cuffed to the table. "When Vic tried to take him downtown, he attacked Vic and went for his gun. So we arrested the idiot. Polk's lucky he didn't get shot."

"Is he working with Schilling?" Webb asked. "Or is Schilling innocent?"

"We don't know yet," Erin said. "But we did find this in his sock drawer." She dangled an evidence bag which contained a pill bottle. They'd given Polk's apartment a good once-over before taking him in.

"And what is that?" Webb asked.

"We'll know for sure when we test it," she said. "But I'm betting it's Rohypnol."

Webb rubbed his face. "Okay, so he had means and opportunity, and past history suggests he's capable of drugging her. I heard from CSU while you were out. They just finished sifting through Schilling's apartment. They found some sketchy stuff, including dealer volumes of coke and marijuana, and some suggestive pictures of the models, but no Rohypnol. If any of the girls in the pics are underage, we'll have him on a child-pornography beef. Schilling has a personal connection to the victim. Neshenko, I want you to go back to the InterContinental. Talk to Caldwell in Security and get back on those tapes. I want you to pay particular attention to how Devers left the dinner. Was she impaired in any way? And then I want you to find out if Schilling was at the hotel the night she was killed. Can you manage that?"

"He broke my nose, not my brain," Vic said. "Sure, I can do it."

"O'Reilly, you and I will talk to Polk," Webb went on. "Schilling's probably climbing the walls by now, but we've got evidence he's a drug dealer, so we'll charge him with that for starters, along with resisting arrest and assaulting an officer. I want proof he was at the hotel before we brace him on the murder. Leave the dog."

"Rolf, *bleib*," Erin said. Rolf settled himself on his haunches and cocked his head, his tail sweeping the floor. The K-9 was feeling pretty good. He'd gotten to bite two bad guys in two days. He was a good boy and he knew it.

Polk was sitting a little funny, favoring one hip. Erin hid a smile at the sight. She and Webb sat down across from the man.

"I got nothing to say to her," Polk said. "She made her dog bite me. That's police brutality."

"I've got testimony from two of my detectives saying you were actively fighting them at the time," Webb said mildly. "They also say you seized one detective's sidearm. Detective O'Reilly could have legally shot you the moment you touched it. She probably would've gotten a medal for doing it. You're still breathing because she exercised restraint."

"I didn't touch his gun," Polk said.

"We have your fingerprints on the weapon," Webb said.

Polk said nothing.

"So as you can see, Mr. Polk, you're in a great deal of trouble," Webb went on. "You're already looking at several years' imprisonment, depending on what charges we file with the DA. If you go down for attempted murder of a police officer, along with the assault charges, you're not going to see the street again for a decade or more."

Webb had Polk's attention. The man had looked surly and uncomfortable before. Now he looked scared.

Webb leaned forward, clasping his hands together and speaking earnestly. "I'd like to help you out of the hole you're in, Mr. Polk. But for me to be able to do that, you have to help me."

"What do you want?" Polk asked.

"Let's start with the drugs," Webb said, still speaking soothingly. Given that Erin was the one who'd arrested the guy, after fighting him, Webb had taken the role of good cop for this interrogation.

"What drugs?"

"The drugs in your sock drawer, dimwit!" Erin snapped, smacking her fist onto the table. Since Webb was good cop, that left her playing bad cop, and she was just fine with sticking it to this idiot.

"Where did you get them?" Webb asked. "I need the name of your dealer."

"I got no dealer," Polk muttered.

Webb sighed and shook his head sadly. "I'm sorry, Mr. Polk. If you don't cooperate, there's nothing I can do for you." He stood up. "I'll have to recommend the DA prosecute to the fullest extent of the law. Good day."

Erin took her cue and stood to follow her boss out of the room.

She wasn't the least bit surprised when Polk called, "Wait!" before Webb had even touched the doorknob. They had him.

"Yes?" Webb inquired politely, turning his head but remaining poised at the exit.

"There's this guy, he works at a drugstore, he knows how to get stuff," Polk said.

"What's this guy's name?" Webb asked. He slid back into his seat. Erin sat down beside him.

"Pete Ward. Works at the place down at the corner of Seventh and Fifth Avenue."

"What kind of stuff can he get?"

"All kinds. Roofies, X, speed, you name it."

"Good, good," Webb said. "Now, did you know Crystal Winters before you saw her at dinner?"

"No! I told you, I only saw her for a second!"

Webb sighed again. "Mr. Polk, you're not being very helpful."

"It's the truth! You gotta believe me! Why would I lie about that?"

"Because she OD'd and got tossed in a fish tank!" Erin barked. Polk jumped, then winced as his weight came down on his damaged hindquarters.

"I know you didn't mean for her to die," Webb said gently. "It was an accident, right? You got the dosage a little wrong. Then she stopped breathing and you panicked. You tried to save her, but you didn't know how. That'll matter to the jury. They'll see you tried to keep her alive. But it didn't work like in the movies and she just lay there. So you knew you had to get rid of the body and wash off any of your skin cells, or your sweat, or anything you'd left on her. But you knew about the security cameras. So you went to the fuse-box and turned off the power to the third floor. That gave you a chance to haul her body into the maintenance room and dump her in with the fish."

"That's not what happened!" Polk protested.

"Then tell me what did happen, Lloyd," Webb said. "What did you do?"

"Nothing! Look, I like girls, okay? But sometimes they need a little encouragement, they want it but they don't know they do. Know what I mean? Girls these days are scared to say what they want, they're all repressed and stuff, but they all want it in the end. That's all the pills are for, to loosen 'em up a little. But I was workin' that night. I never do nothin' with the girls at the hotel. I'd lose my job for that!"

"Your job's the least of your worries," Erin said. "You're facing serious jail time, Polk. Stop jerking us around."

"I'm not!" Polk insisted. "Okay, yeah, they told me about the power outage on Three, so I went to the fuse-box and reset the breaker. But I didn't turn it off in the first place. The breaker was tripped when I got there!"

"You better be sure about that," Erin growled.

"It was already tripped! I swear!"

"Convenient," Erin muttered. "For you."

"When did you get the call about the breaker?" Webb asked.

"Quarter to midnight," Polk said. "Give or take. One of the guests was watching a movie, I guess, and got pissed when it turned off. Security told me to get on it ASAP."

"Who told you to fix it?" Erin asked.

"Our main security guy," Polk said. "Barry Caldwell. And I'm telling you, I never saw that girl, Crystal, once she got on the elevator. Never saw her before, never saw her after."

"Do you have anything else to add?" Webb asked.

Polk thought about it. To Erin it looked like he was trying to come up with something that would get them off his case. "Maybe the old guy in the tux did her," he suggested.

"The guy you said was paying for it?" Erin asked, raising an eyebrow. "Guys don't usually need to roofie hookers."

"I don't know!" Polk exclaimed. "I don't know that guy either! But why aren't you talking to him?"

"You'd throw anybody under the bus to save yourself," Erin said with a deliberate sneer. Then she paused, as if the thought had just struck her. "Who else has access to the fuses?"

"All the maintenance guys," Polk said. "And the security guys. Plus management, but they never go in there. Hey!" He snapped his fingers, making the handcuffs rattle. "Feldspar. The manager."

"What about him?" Erin asked.

"He's a peeping Tom. There's those hidden cameras over the beds in some of the rooms. He doesn't think anybody knows about it, but I do."

"And you're just now telling us this," Erin said, letting him hear the skepticism in her voice.

"Yeah! He sees everything! You wouldn't believe what goes on in hotels!"

"I think we would," Webb said dryly. "Thank you, Mr. Polk. That'll be all for now."

"So, I can go now?" he asked with sudden hope.

"Yeah, you can go," Erin said. "Assuming you can post bail."

"Bail? What for? I didn't kill her!"

"You still broke a cop's nose and had a bottle of illegal drugs behind your socks," she said. "I guess the next time I see you will be at your trial."

"Wait!" Polk shouted. "Wait! I did what you asked!"

"And the judge will take that into consideration," Webb said. "I meant what I said, Mr. Polk. And assuming you've told us the truth, you're in no danger of being charged with murder."

"I need a doctor! I'm gonna get rabies or something!"

"You won't get rabies," Erin said. "Rolf's had all his shots."

"We'll have a doctor brought down to your cell," Webb said. "And some food. You a burger guy?" Food, Erin had learned, was often a good incentive to reward perps for cooperation. It was amazing what a man would do for a bag of fast food, especially after a couple days of jail food.

"Yeah, a cheeseburger would be good," Polk admitted.

* * *

"What do you think?" Webb asked Erin, once they were back in the observation room.

Rolf, tail wagging, looked hopefully at Erin. Maybe she wanted to take another crack at the bad guy. If so, he wanted her to know he'd be right there beside her.

She scratched him behind the ears. "Polk's a date-raping asshole and I'm glad that other woman smacked him down. I'm even gladder Rolf took a chunk out of his ass. He had motive, means, and opportunity. But he also sounds like he's telling the truth. He's a bad guy. I'm just not sure he's our guy. What do you think, sir?"

"I agree," Webb said. "He may have been blowing smoke. On the other hand, I think we want to look a little closer at some of the hotel employees."

"Like Feldspar?" Erin asked.

"Yeah. If he's really got surveillance cameras set up in the rooms, he's got to be a suspect. For all we know, he uses hidden cameras to pick victims. There's a thought. See if there've been any complaints of drugging or sexual assault at the hotel in the past." He held up a hand, stopping Erin's protest before it got out of her mouth. "I know, I know, it's the most underreported crime. But if there's enough of a pattern of behavior, maybe somebody said something. It's worth a look."

"Feldspar could have cut the power," Erin said thoughtfully. "It's a little weird that he'd stash the body where he did. He'd have to know it would look bad for the hotel, and might get him caught."

"This wasn't a deliberate murder," Webb reminded her. "Maybe he panicked. It would've been hard to smuggle the body out of the hotel. Wherever she ended up, he'd have the same problem."

"Sir," Erin said as a thought struck her. "How did the body get from the fifth floor to the third floor?"

Webb blinked. "We don't know where she died," he said. "For all we know, she died in the hallway and the killer just dragged her a few feet."

"What about cameras in the elevators?" she asked.

Webb cursed. "I should've thought of that." He snatched out his phone and poked the screen. It rang a couple of times. "Neshenko?"

There was a short pause in which Vic said something Erin couldn't catch. "While you're looking," Webb said, "check the elevator footage. I need to know if our victim made it downstairs under her own power. Specifically, I need to know how she got to the third floor."

There was a longer pause. Erin imagined Vic complaining about having to look at more hours of security footage. Webb looked tolerant at first, then bored, then irritated.

"Keep me posted if you find anything," Webb finally said and hung up without waiting for an answer.

"I'll get on the hotel's complaint history," Erin said.

"One other thing," Webb said. "Call Judge Ferris. Tell him we need a warrant."

"For what?"

"On second thought, don't bother. Not even Ferris would sign off on this."

"What were you thinking, sir?"

"I was wanting to have a CSU team sweep the hotel for hidden surveillance devices," he said, shaking his head. "There's no way. Too much ground to cover. The hotel won't like it. Imagine if word got out that we were sweeping for mini-cams in their bedrooms. The bad publicity would wreck them. They'd sue the city. And word always gets out. We can't do this solely on the word of a lowlife like Polk. We need more evidence."

"We need evidence so we can collect evidence?" Erin asked with a cynical smile.

"It's just like applying for a job," he said, returning the cynicism with interest. "To get a job, you need two to five years of experience. If you don't have the experience, you can't get the experience. That's the way of the world."

"It's amazing anything ever gets done, sir," she said. "I'll see what I can dig up."

* * *

Back upstairs at her desk, Erin looked through the history of criminal complaints from the hotel. Webb was at his computer collating information, looking for patterns. Erin found the usual stuff: noise complaints, disorderly conduct, and petty theft for the most part. She did find an assault charge, but that had been a guy who'd gotten drunk and hit his wife. Nobody had filed a statement claiming they'd been drugged or sexually assaulted.

That didn't mean it hadn't happened. As Webb had pointed out, rape was chronically underreported. If the victim had been drugged through someone spiking her drink, she might not even have understood exactly what had happened. She might have assumed she'd had a blackout on account of the alcohol, and if she'd known she'd had intercourse, she might have believed she'd consented to it.

"You should've bit Polk on the balls instead of the backside," she told Rolf.

Rolf cocked his head and wagged his tail. If she was offering a rematch, he was game.

"I think the department would fire me if I trained you to go for the crotch," she said.

Rolf lay back down with a sigh, curling into a ball and tucking his snout under his tail.

Webb's phone rang. "Webb," he said. "Hold on a second, I'm putting you on speaker. O'Reilly, come over here."

Erin got up and hurried to her commander's desk, Rolf right at her heels.

"Go ahead," Webb said.

"Schilling was here, all right," Vic said. "I got him coming into the lobby at eight thirty-two. Looks just like a damn paparazzi. Or is that paparazzo?"

"I don't speak Italian," Webb said. "And I don't care. You mean he's carrying a camera?"

"Yeah."

"He probably came straight from dinner after the photo shoot, like he told me," Erin said. "Except he left this part out."

"He goes upstairs to the ballroom," Vic said. "Camera in the hallway shows him poke his head through the door. A security guy comes up to him, they have some words, Schilling gets mad, stomps off, and leaves."

"He left the hotel again?" Webb pressed. "Before the victim left the ballroom?"

"Yeah. But he must've seen her in there."

"But he left," Webb repeated. "Without drugging her."

"If he cased the place, he might have marked a side door," Erin said. "A service entrance, maybe? He could've snuck back in."

"And he lied to you," Webb said. "I think it's time we had our talk with Mr. Schilling. Neshenko, do you know how the victim got to the third floor yet?"

Vic's sigh was audible over the phone. "Not yet."

"Keep at it," Webb said. "And good work."

"Not a great payoff for doing good work," Erin said after Webb hung up.

"Virtue is its own reward," Webb said. "That's why they pay us so little."

Chapter 9

"I've got rights," Randy Schilling announced, before Webb and Erin had even had the chance to sit down in the interrogation room.

"Of course you do," Webb said agreeably. "And Detective O'Reilly informed you of them when she arrested you. You've got rights, we've got questions."

"The first one is, why did you lie to me?" Erin asked, getting right to the point.

"What the hell are you talking about?" was Schilling's predictable comeback.

"You said you went to a couple of bars after dinner and then you went home," she said. "What you actually did was go to the InterContinental Hotel to spy on your girlfriend."

"How the hell did you know—" Schilling began, then stopped, his brain having apparently caught up with his mouth.

"Security footage," Erin said. "Turns out, in this day and age, you always have to assume someone's watching."

"Privacy is so very twentieth-century," Webb added dryly.

Schilling looked from one of them to the other. He licked his lips. "Okay, okay," he said, resorting to what every guilty man said when caught red-handed. "It's not what it looks like."

"And what does it look like?" Erin inquired.

"I'm not a stalker or anything."

"That sounds like something a stalker might say," Webb said.

"So I heard she was going to this thing at the InterContinental," he said. "And I went there, but only so I could make sure she was okay!"

"You were worried about her safety?" Erin asked, not trying to hide her skepticism.

"Yeah! Hot young girl like her; anything could happen. I mean, she got murdered, didn't she?" Schilling asked with an odd note of triumphant satisfaction that made Erin want to reach over the table and bang his head on it a couple of times.

"You weren't worried about her safety when you beat her up right before she died," she said.

"I never did that! Who the hell told you that?"

"Sarah Devers told us," Erin said. "You hit her in the stomach and you used your fists. You thought that wouldn't leave any marks because there weren't bruises on the skin. I figure you stayed away from her face because she was a model and you didn't want to mark up that pretty face of hers."

He stared at her in disbelief. "How could she tell you that? She's dead!"

"When you hit someone hard in the gut, it bruises the internal organs," Erin said. "A good Medical Examiner can tell."

"And we've got the best one in the city," Webb added.

"You wrote your relationship all over her with your hands," Erin said, letting him hear the disgust in her voice. "Is that why you thought you could take me? Because you think women are weaker than you and you can just do whatever you want with them?"

"That's not... I mean, I didn't... damn it, she just wouldn't leave me alone! She kept on at me about Gloria, and Raquel, and Cindy. It's not like we were exclusive or anything! And I was paying her back, getting her good shots, good exposure. Her whole career was because of me! And then she thinks she can go and screw this other guy, like I'm nothing? I should've busted those perfect teeth of hers. See how many contracts she'd get trying to smile with a mouth full of dentures!"

Webb raised an eyebrow and said nothing.

"Where'd you get the Rohypnol?" Erin asked.

"The what?"

"The roofies. The drug you used to knock her out."

"She never used," Schilling said. "All the other girls do. A little speed, mostly, to keep them perky, maybe some ephedrine to help with the weight. But Sarah wouldn't. That girl was so clean, like her shit didn't stink. God, she was annoying. If she wasn't so smoking hot, I would've cut loose of her by now. I'm glad she's gone."

"You're saying you didn't drug her?" Erin asked.

"I just told you that! You should've seen the look she'd give me at parties. God! What a buzz-kill!"

"You're going to jail, Mr. Schilling," Webb said. "We've got you cold on drug possession. Together with the testimony you've just given, that should be enough to keep you in there for a good long while. If I find out you're lying about drugging Sarah, I can personally guarantee your stay behind bars will be especially unpleasant. I know plenty of people at the Department of Corrections. Some of them work there, some live there because I put them there. So this is your last chance to come clean."

"I've told you everything," Schilling said sulkily. "I went to the hotel, I saw her on the arm of that rich asshat and then that dickless hotel rent-a-cop kicked me out. Then I went out and got drunk."

"Why didn't you just tell me that in the first place?" Erin demanded.

"How was it gonna look? And you think a guy likes to talk about his girl cheating on him? I bet your guy doesn't tell you when he's screwing around behind your back."

"That's because he doesn't," Erin said.

"That's what you think. Every guy cheats."

Webb stood up. "I think we're done here."

Erin followed suit. "Not everybody's like you," she said to Schilling. "Thank God."

* * *

"I need a shower," Erin said as she and her commanding officer walked back up to Major Crimes.

"With bleach," Webb agreed. "I left LA to get away from people like that."

"But you didn't turn in your shield, sir. We meet people like that every shift."

Webb ran a hand through his thinning hair. "Good point. You know, sometimes I get frustrated because we don't have enough suspects."

"And now we've got too many," she said. "I don't think Schilling and Polk were working together."

"No. Both of them are solo acts. Good work getting Schilling to confess to the abuse. If it turns out he's our guy, that'll play well in court."

"Yeah," Erin said. "Except I'm not sure he's our guy. Same with Polk."

"At least it's not a series," Webb said. "Everything points to an accidental overdose."

"He's no serial killer," she said. "He's just a rapist. He's going to keep doing this if we don't stop him."

"I didn't mean it's not serious," Webb said. "I meant... never mind. I'm your commanding officer. I don't owe you explanations. Why don't we take lunch. Sometimes I think better on a full stomach. See you in an hour."

Erin decided to swing by the Barley Corner to grab a bite to eat. Her appetite had returned full force and she wanted some real food, not cheap takeout or vending-machine crap. Plus, she wanted to check on Carlyle. Her brother had said he was in good shape and was likely to make a full recovery, but the Irishman had come within a whisker of death. Erin didn't mean to take any chances.

She and Rolf arrived in the middle of the noon rush. The big-screen TVs were playing a soccer game between teams whose names Erin didn't recognize. She was troubled but not surprised to see Carlyle among the crowd, accompanied by Corky. Carlyle wasn't sitting at his usual place at the bar. In deference to his damaged abdominal muscles, he was in a booth where he could rest his back against something more substantial.

Erin also saw Mickey Connor, flanked by Veronica Blackburn and a pair of rough-looking thugs. They'd cleared a space at the bar. Mickey had a glass of beer in his hand. Everyone else in the place was having a good time watching the game, but Mickey wasn't smiling and wasn't watching the television. He was looking at the other people. Veronica had a hand resting on his meaty forearm. She was dolled up in a tight blouse with a very low neckline and a miniskirt over fishnet stockings. She looked like what she was; a former hooker turned madam.

Mickey's gaze met Erin's across the room. His eyebrows drew down, his eyes narrowing slightly. Without turning his attention away from her, he set his glass on the bar behind him, freeing his hands.

Erin felt a sudden urge to reach for her gun. She'd seen how fast Mickey could move, in spite of his bulk, and she had no doubt he would murder her without a second thought. But she couldn't whip out her Glock and blast him. He wasn't threatening her. He probably wasn't even armed, at least not by the legal definition of the word. She'd heard he carried a roll of quarters in each pocket to add weight to his fists. She thought of trying to explain that to Webb.

"But sir, he had twenty dollars in change. I had to shoot him!"

Someone moved in the corner of her vision, ringing all her internal danger alarms. She didn't want to take her eyes off Mickey, but the movement she'd caught was purposeful, like a predator stalking its prey. She risked a quick glance.

Her breath whooshed out of her in relief. It was Ian Thompson. He'd picked up on the nonverbal exchange between her and Mickey and was moving their way. His coat was unbuttoned, one hand resting easily inside the lapel in a posture any police officer would recognize. He was holding the grip of a pistol in a shoulder holster.

Mickey's eyes flicked Ian's direction. Ian stopped a few yards to Erin's left, forming the third point of a triangle. Ian always moved with tactics in mind. He was flanking Mickey so he and Erin could put him in a crossfire if the big ex-boxer tried anything.

Between Ian on one side of her and Rolf on the other, Erin wasn't scared of Mickey and his hired muscle. She let herself smile slightly when she looked back at Mickey.

Your move, she thought.

Mickey reached back toward the bar, closed his fingers around his glass, picked it up, and took a long, slow drink. He somehow managed to load even that ordinary gesture with menace. It seemed to go on for minutes as he stared at her over the rim of the glass. He didn't blink.

Veronica puckered her puffed lips and blew Erin a silent kiss.

Erin walked past them to Carlyle's booth, deliberately turning her back. It went against her instincts and experience, but she knew Ian was still watching her six. She needed to show she wasn't afraid. But deep down, she was. Mickey Connor unsettled her in a visceral, physical way. She could still remember the way he'd grabbed her after the card game at Evan O'Malley's place, the incredible speed and strength of the man. Erin didn't like feeling helpless, but she knew if she ever came to close quarters with him again, she'd have no chance at all.

"Hey, guys," she said to Carlyle and Corky. She could still feel Mickey's gaze prickling the back of her neck, but she tried to ignore it. "No, don't get up. You're still hurt. Just tell me what's going on."

"Arsenal's playing Hull City," Corky said. "Grand game. FA Cup final it is. They think it's over, and they're nearly right. Arsenal's up three-two, and I've a tidy sum riding on them, so good luck to the lads."

"I'm sure you're not confessing illegal gambling to a law-enforcement officer," she said with a smile, sitting down across from them.

"If you see any coppers, be sure to point them out," he said cheerfully. "They'll not get a thing out of me."

Erin reached across the table and took one of Carlyle's hands. "Should you be up and around?" she asked quietly.

"I need to show the flag," he said. "And I've spent enough time lying about in bed these past days. A football match is just what I'm needing."

"Soccer," Erin gently reminded him. "Football is a totally different sport in America."

"Now that's just mad," Corky said. "We're watching a game where the lads hit the ball with their bloody feet. If that's not football, you can pack me off to Van Dieman's Land. In what you Yanks call football, how often do the lads' feet touch the ball?"

"Kickoff, punting, and field goals," she said.

"And what do they hold it with the rest of the time?"

"Their hands," Erin admitted.

"So why don't you call it handball?" Corky asked triumphantly.

"There's already a sport called handball," Carlyle said.

"And there's a perfectly grand sport called football," Corky retorted, cocking his head toward the nearest TV screen.

"Okay, you win," Erin said. "Football it is."

"Bloody Yanks, renaming all our sports," Corky muttered in mock indignation. "When it comes to sport, your lot are overpaid, oversexed, and overtime."

"You're one to talk about being oversexed," Carlyle said mildly.

Erin snorted.

Caitlin, one of the Corner's waitresses, came over. Erin ordered a Reuben sandwich and a glass of Guinness. Corky favored Caitlin with a wink and a pat on the behind, which earned him a playful swat with the back of her hand. They had a sometimes-thing going.

"And how's the world of policing?" Carlyle asked.

"Got a weird one," Erin said. "The victim's a fashion model. Accidental drug overdose. We think someone tried to slip her a mickey, but something went wrong and she died."

"That's unfortunate, but hardly unusual, sad to say," Carlyle said.

"He left her floating in the aquarium at a fancy hotel," she said.

"That's a mite odd," Corky allowed.

"We've got two main suspects," she went on. "One's a dirtbag who likes to drug women in bars. We found some of the drug in his possession and he works at the hotel. The other's her boyfriend. He was abusing her and cheating on her, and he's a drug dealer on the side, but we don't know if he had access to Rohypnol."

"We had a lad come in here a couple years past, trying his hand with that vile stuff," Carlyle said.

"What happened?" Erin asked.

"Caleb handled the situation."

Caleb Carnahan had been the Corner's previous head of security. He'd been savagely beaten and shot to death only a few days ago. Erin was pretty sure Mickey had done it, but she'd actually taken credit with the Mob for the hit. As far as Evan O'Malley was concerned, she'd had Ian kill Caleb for betraying her and Carlyle. Now Carlyle was suggesting Caleb had... what? She could imagine a number of fates for a man who tried to drug a patron in a Mob bar. None of them were pleasant.

"We're missing the camera footage at the hotel," she continued, deciding not to pursue that line of thought. "Somebody cut the power to that floor for a few minutes."

"The killing was an accident, you say?" Carlyle asked.

"He tried to save her life," she said. "That'll help him if it comes to a plea bargain, but it's still murder."

"Aye," he said thoughtfully. "It just strikes me that thinking to turn off the lights and cameras isn't characteristic of a lad who's panicking. This is a careful thinker you've got here. I'll warrant it's a lad who's gotten away with things in the past, probably so cleverly he's not crossed paths with the coppers before."

"That doesn't help us," Erin said. "I can't look for suspects on the basis of them *not* having criminal records."

"Do either of these suspects of yours have a history of impulsive, reckless acts?"

"Both of them," she said ruefully. "You're saying both guys sound wrong for this?"

"You're saying that," he said. "You know the situation better than I. Were I looking to solve this, I'd be trying to puzzle out how the lass was drugged, where she was, and what happened to her after. Where was she?"

"Somewhere in the hotel. She went upstairs with her dinner date to his room. He said she left about eleven."

"And you trust this lad?" Carlyle asked.

"I don't trust anybody," she said.

"There's our fine lass," Corky said approvingly. "You've been teaching her well, Cars."

"We know she left the dinner at the ballroom," Erin said. "And she probably went to the guy's room. That's all we know for sure. At some point she got drugged and her heart stopped. Someone, not a professional, tried to give her CPR. Then that person, or maybe another one, cut the power, smuggled her into a back room, and dumped her body."

"What would the lad have needed in order to do that?" Carlyle asked.

"He'd have needed keys to the electrical room. And to the room with the fish tank." She paused. "He needed to know the hotel layout. He wouldn't have had time to figure all of it out once she was dead. He'd have wanted to get rid of the body as fast as possible."

"Nay, lass," Carlyle said. "He needed none of those things. He only needed one thing."

"What's that?"

"Money."

"What does money have to do with this?" she retorted.

"Everyone's got a price," Carlyle said. "Corky, how would you go about disposing of an unexpected corpse in a fancy hotel?"

"I'd tip the housekeeper extra to get rid of it," Corky said, without a moment's hesitation.

"Are you saying the housekeeper's in on it?" Erin asked, not sure if he was joking or not.

"He's saying it's easier to pay someone who already knows something, and has access, than to do it all oneself," Carlyle said. "He's saying most lads can be bought. You're not looking for someone with access to the hotel. You're looking for someone with access to your poor departed colleen. Then you're looking for someone with the proper keys and knowledge who can be bought. Do you know anyone like that?"

Erin stood up. "Yeah, I think I do," she said. "Thanks, guys."

"Half a moment, darling," Carlyle said with a smile. "You've a sandwich on the way."

"You can't go saving the city while you're starving to death," Corky added. "Your figure's in no need of dieting." He gave her an appreciative look. "Join us."

Erin's stomach rumbled, as if on cue. Rolf cocked his head at her. He was in favor of chasing bad guys, but he was also in favor of food.

She sat down again. "Okay. But then I have to get moving. And leave my figure out of this, Corky."

"Never," Corky said, winking.

"That's my woman you're discussing," Carlyle said.

"A lad can look and dream," Corky said. "Even if he's not allowed anything more."

Chapter 10

"I'm not coming back to the Eightball, sir," Erin said into her phone. She was on the road again, behind the wheel of her Charger, after a good but hurried meal.

"Resigning?" Webb asked wryly.

"In your dreams, sir," she said. "I have a lead. I'm going back to the hotel. What if the killer didn't handle things himself? What if he paid someone on staff to help him?"

"This wasn't premeditated," Webb reminded her.

"That's not what I mean. This is an upscale hotel. They handle problems for their guests."

"O'Reilly, if you're suggesting the hotel moved our victim's corpse as some sort of courtesy..."

"No, sir. I'm just saying it's a service industry, and body disposal is a service. At least, that's how our guy might have seen it. For the right price."

"Okay, see what you can find. Keep me posted."

Erin arrived at the InterContinental and walked quickly in, Rolf trotting beside her. He'd picked up on her energy and knew they were in the hunt. The K-9's nostrils twitched in anticipation.

She found Vic in the security station, still poring over surveillance videos, a white Chinese takeout box and a bottle of Mountain Dew beside him. His face was badly swollen, both his eyes blacked. It was a common symptom of a broken nose. Barry Caldwell was sitting nearby, sipping a cup of coffee.

"Hey, Vic," she said. "Crack the case yet?"

"I'm gonna crack *something* in a couple minutes," he said. "I got nothing. Seriously. She gets on the elevator with Stone a little after nine. She doesn't come back down."

"Is there any chance anyone could have manipulated this film?" Erin asked Caldwell.

"I don't see how," he said. "The security station always has a guy on duty. If he has to step away, the door is locked."

"So one of your security people could have done it?" she pressed.

"All my people are good people," Caldwell said. "Nobody screwed with the film. Look at it!"

"I've been looking at it," Vic growled. "I've got pixels burned into my eyeballs. But I've checked the time stamps. No gaps. I'm telling you, our victim doesn't come down the elevator."

"The stairs, then," Erin said.

Vic shook his head wearily. "You think I didn't check them?"

"Fire escape?" she guessed.

"Alarms go off if you open the fire doors," Caldwell said.

"Of course they do," Erin said. "Unless someone turns them off. But I suppose you'd need access to security systems to do that."

"Exactly what are you suggesting, Detective?" Caldwell asked.

"I'm suggesting this crime was impossible," she said, looking him in the eye. "Unless the killer had access to security systems."

"My people had nothing to do with this," he said.

"I didn't say that. The killer just would have needed an understanding with someone who could get at the security systems."

"And I'm telling you again, all my people are good people," Caldwell shot back. "I know you active-duty officers look down on rent-a-cops, but they're well trained. I got a couple former NYPD guys here and two Army veterans. If any of them were into anything, I'd know about it."

"Yeah, you probably would," Erin agreed. "But there's one person who had access you can't vouch for."

"Yeah? Who's that?"

Erin held his eye and didn't say anything. She was looking for weakness, for him to look away.

Caldwell blinked. "You don't seriously mean—" he began.

"Makes sense," Vic said. He'd been watching the exchange, a welcome break from the security footage. "You could've tripped the breakers. You also could've turned off a fire alarm. Hell, you could've made the whole system do whatever you wanted. Nobody's looking over your shoulder. What's that old saying about watchmen, Erin?"

"'Who watches the watchmen?'" Erin quoted.

Caldwell looked angry now, angry and a little scared. "I don't know what the hell you're talking about," he said. "I've been helping you!"

"Best way to avoid suspicion," Erin said quietly. "I know you didn't kill her, Barry. But I also know you probably know who did. Point us in the right direction. You're not the one we want."

"I can't," Caldwell said. "Because I don't know who you want."

"I think maybe you do," Vic said. He stood up and stepped next to Erin.

"You guys are nuts," Caldwell said. "What, so a guy hangs up his shield, because of an injury he got in the line of duty for God's sake, and you turn on him? Jesus! What's the matter with you?"

"This has nothing to do with you having been a cop," Erin said. "One way or the other."

"You big, fancy detectives," he sneered. "You think you're better than me, just because somebody spray-painted your shields gold? What, you gonna pin this on me because I don't have some big friend downtown? Or is it because I worked Vice? You ain't any different. Yeah, you think I don't know how a hot number like you makes detective? Who'd you screw to get that shiny shield, *Detective* O'Reilly?"

"Watch it, asshole," Vic snarled.

"Easy, Vic," Erin said out of the side of her mouth. "I've got this."

"You've got nothing," Caldwell snapped. "And I still have a job to do. Get out of my office. You want to come back, come back with a court order. I have to go."

"You know something I've picked up in interrogations?" Erin asked. "Guilty guys always want to stop the conversation. They want you to shut up and go away. Innocent guys want to explain themselves. They want to clear their names. You want to clear your name, Barry?"

"What'd you do, take psych classes at community college?" Caldwell said. "You got no idea what's going on in my head. And I'm not telling you shit. What, you think I'm stupid? Suppose you're right. Suppose I took a payoff from some rich asshole to cover for him. You think it'll do me a bit of good to give you his name? He goes down for murder, I go down as an accessory. Even if I get off, I still lose my job, and good luck getting another."

"That would've been a good thing to think about before taking the money," Erin said. "And I didn't say anything about a rich asshole. What do you think, Vic?"

"I think our guy Caldwell here is covering for one of his hotel's guests," Vic said. "And I think I can guess which one."

"Last one to see our victim alive?" Erin suggested.

"That's what I'm thinking, yeah."

"You think he'll throw Barry here under the bus to try to save himself?"

"It's what I'd do in his place."

"And poor Barry can't afford a fancy lawyer," Erin said. "Maybe our rich asshole beats the rap and leaves Barry to take the heat."

"That's cold," Vic said. "But yeah, I could see it happening. What do you think, Barry?"

"I think if you're arresting me, go for it," he said. "And if you are, I'm exercising my right to an attorney. If you're not, shut up and get out. Either way, this conversation's over."

Erin knew they didn't have nearly enough to charge Caldwell with anything. But she also knew that if he was guilty, and she thought he was, they couldn't leave him running the security office at the hotel. He'd be looking for ways to destroy any remaining evidence linking him to Sarah's death. So they really didn't have a choice.

She pulled out her handcuffs. "Have it your way. Barry Caldwell, you're under arrest as an accessory to murder after the fact in the killing of Sarah Devers. You have the right to remain silent..."

"You'll regret this, Detective," was the only thing Caldwell said when she finished reading him his rights.

"Wouldn't be the first time," Erin said.

"Stone next?" Vic suggested.

"Let's do it," she said.

"I think we should have a hotel security guy with us," he said. "For diplomatic reasons."

"Great idea," she said. "Come on, Barry. Little detour before we go back to the Eight. You're coming with us."

They loaded him into the elevator and rode up to the fifth floor. Caldwell stayed quiet. He was experienced enough to know that any protests or arguments were only likely to get him in more trouble. Rolf kept an eye on the handcuffed man. Just because he hadn't needed a show of teeth didn't mean it was out of the question.

"I'm sure you've thought this through," Vic said conversationally. "But we don't have a warrant to search Stone's room."

"Not yet," Erin agreed.

"You're the Detective Second Grade," he said. "I'm just along for the ride."

At Stone's door, Erin paused to listen. She heard nothing. She rapped sharply with her knuckles.

"Mr. Stone!" she called. "This is the NYPD. We need to talk to you again."

Silence answered her.

She gave it a moment and tried once more. Nothing.

"When I'm traveling," Caldwell said, "I always stay in my hotel room in the middle of the afternoon instead of seeing the sights, visiting people, going to museums..."

"Shut up," Vic said. To Erin, he added unnecessarily, "I don't think anyone's home."

That made the visit upstairs a bust. They couldn't go into the hotel room without a warrant, and Erin didn't think having their security chief in handcuffs on an iffy accessory charge would put the rest of the hotel staff in a cooperative mood.

"Let's get this guy back to the Eightball," she said. "We'll sort out Stone soon enough."

On the way out of the hotel, as they were walking past the concierge's desk, Erin had a thought. Signaling Vic to stay put with Caldwell, she and Rolf hurried over to the desk.

"May I help you, ma'am?" the concierge asked.

"I'm looking for Wendell Stone," she said. "He's up in 503."

"I'm sorry, ma'am," he said. "Mr. Stone checked out just a little while ago. He's no longer registered here."

Erin clenched her jaw and her fists. "Thank you," she said through gritted teeth. He could be halfway to Boston by now, well out of the NYPD's jurisdiction.

*   *   *

"Just one question, O'Reilly," Webb said. "Are you intending to arrest everybody involved with this case? Because if so, we're going to need to call over to the Nine and borrow some space in their holding cells."

"Just one more, sir," Erin said.

"Who?" Webb looked from her to Vic. They hadn't bothered putting Caldwell in an interrogation room. He'd lawyered up the second they stepped into the station, so they'd just stuffed him in lockup before coming upstairs to face their commanding officer.

"Wendell Stone," she said.

"The Third," Vic added.

"That'll make four suspects in custody," Webb said. "They can't all have killed Miss Devers."

"I think Stone killed her," Erin said. "And he paid off Caldwell to help cover it up."

"And you know this how, exactly?"

"Sergeant Brown says Caldwell was on the take when he worked Vice."

Webb stared at her. "And?"

"And Stone needed someone to take down the cameras on the third floor. Along with maybe turning off the fire alarms or messing with the elevator cameras."

"That's it? You arrested a former police officer for *that*?"

Webb hadn't raised his voice, but his tone grew harder as he ended the sentence.

"This guy's dirty, sir," Vic said. "Erin's right."

"Oh, good, both my detectives are in on this together," Webb said. "I assume you have proof, not just a hunch?"

"We'll get the proof," Erin said.

"How reassuring." Webb didn't look reassured. "I assume Caldwell's lawyer is on the way?"

"First thing he asked for," Vic said.

"How do you know Stone killed Devers?"

"I don't, sir," Erin said. "Not for certain. But I think he did."

"I'm sure the DA will be very pleased to hear that. What about the other two?"

"Schilling and Polk?" Erin asked.

Webb nodded.

"We've got Schilling as a drug dealer and Polk for possession of an illegal drug and assaulting an officer," she said. "It's enough to charge both of them."

"I know about that already." Webb twirled an unlit cigarette in his fingers and looked at it with dull, hopeless longing. "But you're saying they're not part of this case?"

"I don't think so."

"You sure you don't want to arrest anyone else?"

"I'd kind of like to get Feldspar," Vic said.

Webb actually laughed, a rare sound in Major Crimes. "I can't wait to see your DD-5s. By the time you two are done, the number of people in this case you haven't arrested will be smaller than the number you have. Why don't you arrest that Latina housekeeper, whatever her name is, while you're at it?

The one who found the body? She's probably in trouble with ICE if nothing else."

"I don't work for Immigration," Vic said stiffly.

"Neither do I," Erin chimed in. Both of them had soft spots for hardworking immigrants, whether their green cards were in order or not.

"I was joking," Webb said. "So, you want Feldspar on suspicion of hiding cameras in hotel rooms?"

"That's right, sir," Vic said.

"On the word of Polk," Webb said. "A guy who'd sell his own mother to get out of trouble. You need more, if you want any of this to stick."

"What do you need from us, sir?" Erin asked.

"Hard evidence. An eyewitness who saw Sarah Devers with one of these guys. A pill bottle in the hotel. DNA. Fingerprints. Something. Because right now, you've got a lot of supposition, assumptions, hunches, and hot air. God, I could use a smoke right now."

"We need to bring in Stone," Erin said. "We can break him in interrogation. I'll tell him Caldwell flipped on him."

"Long shot, O'Reilly," Webb said, shaking his head. "If he calls your bluff, you've got nothing."

"You're forgetting we don't know where he is," Vic said. "He's probably not even in the state anymore. Good luck getting him extradited from Massachusetts on something this flimsy."

"Maybe he's not there yet," she said slowly. "He's not flying and he's not driving."

"What do you mean?" Webb asked.

"He said he preferred to travel by rail," she said. "He'd be going from Penn Station. Maybe he hasn't left yet."

"Amtrak tends to run in the evenings," Vic said, rushing over to his computer and bringing up the train schedule. He quickly scanned the timetables. "Looks like the next train to Boston isn't until five o' clock."

Erin checked the clock. They'd lost a lot of the afternoon going back and forth from the InterContinental and booking Caldwell. It was almost four thirty. "We don't have much time," she said. "Let's go."

"You two go on," Webb said. "I'd just slow you down. I'll call the station and see if I can line up some uniforms to help."

"I always wanted to grab a perp in a train station," Vic said as they jogged down the stairs to the parking garage. "You know that scene in *The Untouchables*? The shootout at Union Station?"

"I didn't know you wanted to be Kevin Costner," Erin said, throwing open the door to the garage. Rolf was prancing beside her, tail whipping back and forth. He knew a chase when he saw one.

"Not Costner," Vic said. "Andy Garcia. That moment when he catches the baby carriage with one hand and shoots the guy with the other? Pure gold. I bet you wanted to be Sean Connery."

"Why do you say that?"

"He's the Irish cop."

"Sean Connery is Scottish." She pulled out her keys and opened the back compartment. Rolf leaped in.

"But he's playing an Irish guy. Same thing." Vic slid into the passenger seat as Erin took her place behind the wheel.

"It is not the same thing! It's completely different!" She cranked the key in the Charger's ignition. "How would you like to be mistaken for, I don't know, a Ukrainian?"

"Okay, fair point."

"And Vic? Try not to shoot anybody today."

"Hey, if he pulls a gun, all bets are off."

"Forget Rolf," she said. "We ought to put a leash on *you*."

Chapter 11

"Fifteen minutes to the train station, give or take," Erin said.

Vic glanced at the dashboard clock. "We've got less than thirty. Should I get out and push?"

"If it'll make you feel better."

Traffic wasn't too bad by Manhattan standards. Erin turned on the lights and siren, which helped as long as there was room for the other cars to get out of the way. That got them as far as West Twenty-First Street, where they ran into hard gridlock.

"Damn, damn, damn," Erin muttered, craning her neck to try to see around the cars that blocked them.

"I see some other flashers up there," Vic said. "Looks like an accident at the light."

Erin sagged back in her seat. "Great."

"There's always the sidewalk," Vic suggested.

"That's one way to turn in your shield," she said.

"Hey, if you're gonna go, go big," he said. "Hang tight for a sec."

He unbuckled his seatbelt and stepped out onto the pavement. Giving her a nod, he ran on ahead, threading his way through the stalled traffic.

"Well, here we are," Erin told Rolf. "I didn't think he'd actually get out."

Rolf thrust his nose through the hole next to Erin's head and panted.

The minutes ticked away. Erin pictured their guy, settled comfortably in a first-class Amtrak car, enjoying a leisurely getaway. And there wasn't a damned thing she could do about it from here. They were boxed in behind and on both sides.

Maybe she should call Webb, see if they could get some uniforms to grab Stone. She reached for her phone.

The cars in front of her shifted slightly. Erin sat up and gripped the steering wheel more tightly.

The jam was breaking up. As the path opened, like the Red Sea parting for the Israelites, Erin saw Vic waving cars down a garage ramp, windmilling his arm.

Erin pulled alongside. Vic abandoned his spot on the blacktop and hopped in before the car had stopped rolling.

"Hit it," he said.

She obliged. "And here I thought you didn't want to be a traffic cop," she said.

He scowled. "Don't you dare tell anyone back at the Eightball, or I'll be pulling DayGlo vests out of my locker for months."

"How'd you swing it?" she asked.

"That garage exits onto Twenty-First," he explained. "I came to an understanding with the parking attendant."

"Those guys aren't too understanding in my experience," she said doubtfully. "You didn't bribe him, did you?"

"Nah. I might've implied we were trying to stop terrorists from blowing up the Empire State Building."

"Told him he'd be a big hero, et cetera?"

"Something like that."

"You're a terrible person, Vic."

"Terrible people get shit done."

"We ought to put that on our business cards." Erin accelerated as much as she dared. They'd lost ten minutes. It'd be close.

*   *   *

Erin came in hot, laying rubber on the street outside Penn Station. She slid into one of the police spots on Seventh Avenue. She, Vic, and Rolf were out and running before the pair of startled uniformed officers curbside could do more than gape. She held up her shield so they wouldn't get tackled by some overzealous transit cop.

They sprinted through the New Jersey Transit waiting area to the main concourse and the Amtrak ticketing. Erin was struck by the contrast. The NJ Transit hub was standing-room only, packed with commuters on their way home. The Amtrak area was at least as big and nearly deserted. In the space of a few running strides, the detectives went from rush hour to a practically empty hall where their shoes echoed hollowly on the tile.

"Where's the train to Boston?" she snapped at one of the bored-looking attendants at the counter.

"There's only the one track," the clerk replied. "West Side Line." He pointed with his thumb. "But they're leaving any second."

She didn't bother to answer. Vic was already moving. Rolf pranced impatiently. Erin raced to catch up, silently blessing all those early-morning jogs in Central Park. Running through the empty station, she remembered the abandoned subway tunnel she and Vic had entered the previous year. That case had culminated in gunfire and explosions.

They spilled out onto the boarding platform next to the sleek silver train. The deep thrum of the massive diesel engines made the concrete vibrate under their shoes. The carriages were beginning to move.

"You wanted a movie moment," she gasped to Vic.

The big Russian put on an extra burst of speed and jumped, grabbing the handrail on the last car and pulling himself onto the step. He turned and reached back. Rolf, at her side, was running easily, not even breathing hard.

"Rolf! *Hupf!*" she ordered. Without breaking stride, the Shepherd coiled his spine and jumped. Vic snagged the K-9's vest by the handle just behind the collar and swung Rolf onto the train.

Erin was right on his heels. The train was picking up speed. She put her head down and ran flat-out. Taking a deep breath, she leaped and reached.

Vic's hand closed around her forearm. She clamped her own grip on his wrist and let him reel her in. Then the three of them were together, crammed tight at the end of the passenger car.

"You good?" Vic asked.

"Yeah. You?"

"I think I need to ease up on the weights at the gym," he said. "And do some cardio."

"Good thing Webb didn't come along, huh?" Erin said.

"Yeah." Vic snickered between breaths. "He'd have had a coronary right there on the platform."

"What the hell is going on?" a man demanded.

Erin and Vic turned to face a conductor.

"That's dangerous, what you just did," he went on. "You could've been badly hurt, or even killed."

"NYPD," Erin said, holding up the shield she hadn't bothered to clip back on her belt. "Where's the first class section?"

"Right behind the cabin, up front," he said.

"So, all the way at the other end," Vic said. "Typical."

"You can't go between cars while the train is in motion," the conductor said. "Except in emergencies or..." Then he paused.

"Or when directed by a police officer?" Erin inquired sweetly.

"Yeah," he muttered. "I guess you're okay. Just be careful you don't fall off."

The train had so few passengers that Erin wondered why they bothered to keep running it. The nation's passenger lines operated on a mix of nostalgia and government subsidies. It was too bad. She'd always liked trains; the big, strong, industrial feel of the engines coupled with the glamor of smooth, easy travel. No stoplights, no gas stations, just a straight shot to the destination.

They made their way to the front of the train, ignoring the odd looks and questions from the few onlookers. It really wasn't difficult to move from one carriage to the next. The only reason it was forbidden was so some idiot's next-of-kin wouldn't be able to sue the railroad if they took a header after one too many drinks. Erin and Vic were too sober, and Rolf too sure-footed, to be in any danger.

The first-class carriage was just like the first-class cabin on an airplane; the same metal tube as everyone else, just bigger and better seats.

"Fat cats need more leg room, I guess," Vic said.

The carriage contained two guys in business suits, an elderly couple, a train attendant, and a familiar face half-hidden behind the Wall Street Journal.

"Mr. Stone," Erin said, walking briskly toward him.

If he was startled, Wendell J. Stone III hid it well. He carefully folded the paper and set it on the table in front of him. "If it isn't the young lady from the hotel! What an unexpected pleasure. Do come sit down. I was about to order a cocktail. Would you like anything?"

He signaled to the attendant with a lazy wave of his finger. She arrived at his seat at about the same time Vic, Erin, and Rolf did.

"I'll have a dry martini," Stone said. "And for the young lady...?"

"Isn't there a drink called an aquarium?" Erin asked, watching Stone. He blinked, but didn't flinch.

"I'm sorry, ma'am," the attendant said. "I'm not familiar with that. We don't have a very well-stocked bar."

"Rum, Curaçao, and lemon juice," Vic said, earning him a surprised glance from Erin. "What? I hung out at bars a lot back in school. Still do."

Erin was hardly one to talk. She turned her attention back to Stone. "We need to discuss some things, sir."

"Then sit down, by all means," he said. "I'm sorry we don't have a seat for your colleague. He will simply have to place himself across the aisle."

"Fine by me," Vic grunted. He took a seat, from which he glared at Stone. It wasn't that he was trying to be intimidating; Vic came across that way by default. His appearance was even more alarming on account of the elbow to the nose Polk had given him the day before. The dark swellings under his eyes forced them into a narrow, hard stare.

Erin sat opposite Stone, the table between them. "Rolf, *sitz*," she ordered. The K-9 promptly sat. She watched Stone's face and hands. The face might give something away and the hands might go for a weapon. Neither she nor Stone took any notice of the train attendant, who departed.

"I must say, Miss... O'Reilly, wasn't it?"

"*Detective* O'Reilly."

"Yes, of course. Detective, you must have been simply frantic to see me again, to go to the trouble of hopping a train all the way to Boston."

"I'm not going to Boston. Neither are you."

Stone raised a polite eyebrow. "I would suggest, Detective, that one of us may have taken the wrong train."

"We talked to Caldwell," she said.

"I don't know any Caldwell, I'm sorry to say."

"Maybe you didn't get his last name. But he had plenty to say about you."

Stone spread his hands. "Really, Detective, I hate to disappoint you, but I truly have no idea to whom you are referring."

"Forty-something guy with a limp and a hotel security uniform? Does that jog your memory?" Erin looked for a flicker of anything in Stone's eyes. They were as empty as the Amtrak concourse.

"The guy you had turn off the cameras on the third floor," Vic said.

"I'm sorry, Detectives, I can't help you."

"You drugged Sarah Devers," Erin said.

"Sarah who?"

"Sarah Devers." Erin was suddenly angry, wanting to shake this smug, rich jerk until his teeth rattled. "She called herself Crystal Winters, but she had a real name, and hopes, and a life, and you took them away from her. Why? Was it because she wouldn't put out for you?"

"There's no call to be rude, Miss O'Reilly," Stone said, raising a hand. "I understand you're upset. It's a terrible thing, what happened to that girl. A tragedy. But it has nothing to do with me."

"You thought she was a hooker," Erin went on. "Because she worked for a modeling agency and you hired her to look pretty on your arm. But then she wouldn't go the rest of the way with you. The only thing that surprises me is that you had the drugs already on you."

"I don't use drugs," Stone said. "Well, that's not entirely accurate. I do have a slight hypertensive condition, for which I take a medication."

"The Rohypnol makes it premeditated sexual assault," Erin said softly. "That stuff's only good for one thing, and every judge and district attorney knows it."

"You'll find I had no intimate contact with the late Miss... Devers, was it?"

"Because she died before you could rape her," Erin said, speaking louder now. The elderly couple turned in their seats to look at them. The woman whispered something in her companion's ear.

"Again, Miss O'Reilly, you're being rude," Stone said. "I have been forbearing, but really, I must ask you to moderate your tone."

"Moderate this," Erin said. "If you'd called an ambulance when she stopped breathing, you'd be looking at manslaughter, tops. Along with violation of the Controlled Substances Act, of course. And it's *Detective* O'Reilly."

"Ah," Stone said. "Are you accusing me of a crime, Detective?"

"Several. After covering up the death, you're facing a first-degree murder charge. That means we lock you up for how long, Vic?"

"The rest of your life," Vic helpfully supplied.

"Well, in that case, I have to question your jurisdiction," Stone said. "You see, we are aboard an Amtrak train, which falls under the federal aegis."

"Good thing it's called the *Federal* Controlled Substances Act," Erin said. "The drugs make this a national crime."

"Nonetheless, Detective, you'll need to discuss this with the Amtrak Police. I'm afraid it's illegal for you to arrest me on board this train. Or, of course, once I debark in Boston. You can, of course, take the matter up with the Boston Police Department. Their chief is an old friend of the family."

"How about if I throw your ass off the train?" Vic suggested. "Then you'll be back on New York soil in a hurry, once you stop bouncing. If you're really lucky, you'll land on your feet."

"And now you're threatening physical violence?" Stone inquired. "Really? What is your name and badge number, Detective?"

The attendant came down the aisle bearing a tray. "Excuse me, please," she said. She set a martini glass in front of Stone and a glass containing a ghastly blue liquid in front of Erin.

"What is this?" she asked.

The attendant looked flustered. "An aquarium, ma'am. I looked up the recipe. I hope I got it right. Is there anything else?"

"I'll be ordering dinner shortly," Stone said. "The salmon, I think, but I should like to see the menu."

"Do you have a railroad police officer on board?" Erin asked the attendant.

"Yes, he's in the baggage car, I think."

"Could you fetch him, please?" Erin figured everyone in the conversation was probably bluffing. It was time to call his.

"Certainly, ma'am. What's the problem?"

Erin showed her shield. "Police business."

The attendant nodded. "Just a moment, ma'am." She hurried off.

"Now then," Erin said. "You were saying?"

"Speaking of menus," Stone said. "I'm aware of a wide buffet of legal options available to me. A harassment suit will be first, naturally. I am also on good terms with the chief editor of the Journal," he indicated the folded newspaper, "and the Boston

Globe. One hates to see good police officers tried in the court of public opinion, so I rather hope we can stop before we get to that disagreeable point."

"So now he's threatening us?" Vic asked. The idea amused him.

"Yeah," Erin said. "So, for the record, Mr. Stone, you're saying you did not give any controlled substance to Sarah Devers?"

"I asked the young woman to my room for a drink and some light conversation, as I previously told you."

"She was underage," Vic observed.

"Not to my knowledge," Stone said.

"And you're saying you didn't take her body to the aquarium on the third floor?" Erin asked.

"Of course not, Detective."

"All right." Erin turned to Vic. "Maybe he's telling the truth."

Vic gave her a look. "You think?"

"I apologize for my earlier rudeness," she said to Stone. "But maybe you're right. We don't want this to get any more unpleasant than it already is."

"That's a good girl," Stone said, in a tone which made Erin want to punch his teeth down his throat. "I knew you could be reasonable. Now, if you'd care to join me for dinner? They really do a surprisingly good job with the salmon in the dining car."

"I might take you up on that," she said. "By the way, where did you learn CPR?"

"I took a first-aid class in my preparatory school," Stone said. "I was on the rowing team and it wasn't beyond the realm of possibility I might be called on to resuscitate some classmate, should he experience a waterborne mishap."

Erin nodded. "Okay. That makes sense."

Then Stone got the look she'd been looking for. It skidded into his eyes like an out-of-control car through a red light. She'd seen it so many times, in the faces of so many perps. It was the look that recognized he'd said something without thinking, that he'd given himself away.

"You were a little out of practice," Erin said. "Makes sense, if you hadn't done it since high school. Your chest compressions were too deep. You cracked some ribs."

"I'm sorry," Stone said, recovering. "To what, precisely, are you referring?"

"What's the problem here, folks?" a new voice called. A cop wearing the uniform of the Amtrak Police was on his way toward them, the attendant hovering behind him.

"Erin O'Reilly, NYPD," she said. "This is Vic Neshenko. We're Major Crimes detectives. This man is wanted for murder."

"You got the warrant?" the cop asked.

"This is a hot pursuit situation," Erin said, which was more or less true.

"Oh." The cop looked uncomfortable. He glanced out the window. The train was really moving now, working its way north by northeast along Manhattan Island. "The next stop isn't until Stamford."

"Where the hell is Stamford?" Vic demanded.

"Connecticut," the cop said.

"Stop this train," Erin said. "Now."

"Ma'am, unless there's an imminent emergency, I can't do that," he said.

"Can we at least arrest this mope?" Vic asked.

"You said he's wanted for murder?"

"And violation of the Federal Controlled Substances Act," Erin added.

The cop looked relieved. "Okay, sure," he said.

"Just a moment," Stone said, starting to rise.

"Sit your ass back in that chair, or I'll put it there for you," Erin snapped.

Startled, Stone did as he was told.

"You can catch the southbound train in Stamford," the cop said. "Or arrange other transportation."

"Look on the bright side," Vic said to Stone as he pulled out his handcuffs. "Looks like you may have time for that salmon after all. But you may have to bend over to eat it, since you won't be using your hands. Hey, Erin, thanks for letting me be good cop this time."

"Vic, you call that being good cop? You called him a mope and threatened to throw him off a moving train."

"Did he really?" the Amtrak cop asked.

Vic grinned. "You think that's something, you should see me when I get to be bad cop."

Chapter 12

Stamford seemed an awfully long way from New York to Erin's mind, but East Coast cities were close together. If the train kept to its normal schedule, they'd be there in less than forty minutes. While Vic kept an eye on Stone, she and the railroad cop retreated to opposite ends of the train car to contact their respective bosses.

"O'Reilly, where are you?" Webb asked without any preliminaries. "I've got uniforms all over Penn Station."

"On my way to Connecticut on the Acela line, sir."

"Connecticut."

"Yes, sir."

"Neshenko with you?"

"Yes, sir."

"And Stone?"

"Yes, sir."

"Did you arrest him?"

"Yes, sir."

"Did he confess?"

Erin sighed. "No, sir. But he did it. I'm sure of it."

"I've been looking into this guy," Webb said. "Wendell J. Stone Junior, that'd be your friend's dad, is a big figure in Massachusetts politics. He's a close personal friend of Billy Bulger. You know who that is?"

"He sounds familiar."

"He should. That's Whitey Bulger's kid brother."

"Whitey Bulger? You're shitting me, sir." Whitey Bulger was probably the most notorious criminal ever to come out of Boston, a racketeer and serial murderer who'd actually operated under the protection of the FBI, thanks to an agent he'd corrupted. He'd been on the run for sixteen years and had only recently been collared and convicted.

"Now, brother Billy was never implicated in any of Whitey's crimes," Webb said. "But he had plenty of power himself when he was President of the State Senate. My point is, the Stones are exceptionally well-connected up in Boston, possibly on both sides of the law. They have political clout and maybe criminal muscle behind them."

"What's that got to do with our guy here?" she asked.

"I assume you haven't let him talk to anybody yet?"

"He'll get his phone call when we book him, same as anybody."

"You can assume his first call will be to his lawyer. That lawyer will get the wheels rolling, and next thing you know, the entire political and legal force of the family will come down on us."

"I'm not scared of lawyers, sir."

"Fear's got nothing to do with it, O'Reilly. What we won't have is time. After he makes his first call, we'll have three or four hours, tops, until some very high-powered attorneys will be posting bail and asking very awkward questions. No matter how high the judge sets bail, our boy will be on the street almost immediately. Do you understand?"

"We need to move fast, sir."

"That's an understatement. You'll have less than half a day to put together an airtight case before he's out of New York again. At that point, it's anyone's guess if we'll even be able to extradite him from Massachusetts. Oh, and his lawyers play dirty."

"How do you know that?" she asked, shooting a quick glance Vic's way to make sure everything was all right. She'd left Rolf with him for moral support. Everything appeared to be in order. Stone was sitting quietly, looking out the window. Vic was watching him closely, probably hoping he'd try something.

"I told you, I've looked into Stone's history," Webb said. "It seems this isn't the first adventure our boy has had in the arena of nonconsensual relationships."

"Really?" Erin had been starting to feel a little droopy. Now a fresh shot of adrenaline hit her system and she was suddenly wide awake again. "I thought he didn't have a record."

"I know a guy back in LA who came there from the BPD," Webb said, referring to the Boston Police Department. "I called him and he talked to some old friends there. It seems Stone has committed several indiscretions, but they've been kept off the books. The women who brought the complaints were discredited, their reputations ruined. One of them lost her job and another had to move out of state. Like I said, these guys play dirty."

"Sir, how could you possibly have heard all that this quickly?" she asked. "That must have taken some time."

"It did." Webb sounded slightly smug. "I called my guy yesterday. He's been working this in the background."

"Why didn't Vic and I know about this?"

"Because the name on my desk has 'Lieutenant' in front of it and yours just says 'Detective,'" he said. "I was playing a hunch. I didn't know if it would pan out. I expect you to tell me what you're up to. It doesn't have to go both ways."

"Of course, sir," Erin said, slightly chastened. "But that won't help us get a conviction. It all sounds like hearsay."

"It is. But it tells me you've probably got the right guy. So get him back to our city and park his entitled backside in one of our holding cells. Get down here as fast as you can."

"I might be able to catch a southbound train," she said doubtfully. "Or we can rent a car, I guess. Or... wait, forget about it. I have an idea."

"Whenever I hear that these days, I get this feeling in my stomach," Webb said. "I used to think it was indigestion, but now I think it's just you and Neshenko giving me heartburn. Don't tell me, I don't want to know. Just get it done."

"Thank you, sir. I'll call you once we hit Manhattan again."

"I'll be at the Eightball. All night, probably." Webb sighed heavily. "Just don't do anything that'll make the evening news, please."

"Copy that, sir."

Erin hung up but didn't put her phone away. She dialed the number of the burner phone Carlyle was currently using.

"Evening, darling," Carlyle answered. She heard the normal background noise of the Corner filtering through the phone.

"Evening," she said. "Sorry to bother you."

"You're never a bother. What is it you're needing?" He'd picked up on her tone and got straight to business.

"I need to get in touch with Corky."

"Well, you're in luck. The lad's right here, practically at my elbow. He's chatting up my waitress and keeping her from doing her job. Half a moment." There was a brief pause, then Erin heard his voice more faintly. "Corky, lad, get your hands off Caitlin and come over here. I've a lass who's wanting to bend your ear."

After a moment, Corky's bright, cheerful voice came on the line. "Evening, love."

"Corky, you don't even know who this is," she said. "Love seems a bit optimistic, even for you."

"Erin! I thought it might be you. Finally decided to move on from this tired old lad and trade in for a superior model?"

"Not exactly. I need a favor. It's short notice."

"What can I do for you?"

"I need a car."

"Easiest thing in the world, love. I know a lad. Any particular make or model?"

"Corky! I don't want you to steal one!"

There was a momentary silence. "I'm not precisely certain why you're calling me, in that case," he said.

"I'm going to be in Stamford, Connecticut in a half hour or so. You've got connections in the transport business. I need a ride back to Manhattan, ASAP."

"Grand," Corky said without a moment's hesitation. "I know just the lad. Where can he find you?"

"Train station. It'll be me, Vic, Rolf, and one other guy, so make sure it's a big car."

"No fear, love. I'll just need to make a quick call to the Teamsters Local 145. I'm on good terms with those lads. They'll send someone."

"Will I need cash in hand?"

"Don't worry your head, love. I'll handle the details. I do business with these lads all the time. They'll be having someone coming down this way regardless. I'll just ask them to make a bit of extra room. It may not be the most comfortable ride, but they'll get you here swift, safe, and sound."

"How will I know your guy?" she asked.

"He'll drop my name. Enjoy your ride, love."

"I owe you one, Corky."

"Just give me a kiss when I see you again and we'll call it even."

He hung up before Erin could object. She stared at her phone and shook her head. Corky was never going to change.

She rejoined Vic and Rolf in their vigil over the prisoner. Vic raised an eyebrow.

"What's up?" he asked.

"I've organized a ride back to New York."

"Connecticut State Patrol?" he guessed.

"Not exactly."

*　　*　　*

"So, who are we looking for?" Vic glanced around the train station. The platform was basically empty.

"He'll know us," Erin said with more confidence than she felt.

"I'd like to make the telephone call to which I'm legally entitled," Stone said.

"You'll get your phone call," Erin said. "You haven't been processed yet."

"Processed, as in bologna?" Stone suggested. "I feel I'm being treated rather like lunch meat at present."

"Exactly like," Vic said. Then his attention sharpened. "Erin! Eyes right!"

Erin spun, reflexively dropping a hand to her Glock. Vic's instincts were good. The guy who was walking toward them looked like trouble. Six-foot two and probably weighing close to two-fifty, he had a handlebar mustache and hard, cold eyes. She looked at his hands, which were in plain view and empty, but she noted a jailhouse tattoo of a spider web on the back of his wrist and the sort of scars a man got on his knuckles from a lifetime of brawling.

"That's close enough, buddy," Vic said when the guy was about twenty feet away. Vic's hand, like Erin's, was resting on the grip of his sidearm. The law-enforcement principle at work was the infamous twenty-one-foot rule; if someone was within that distance and armed, even if it was just a knife, that person was considered an imminent threat.

"Easy, cowboy," the big guy said, putting up a hand. "I'm lookin' for Erin. Corky sent me."

Erin relaxed and let go of her pistol. Vic didn't.

"I'm Erin," she said. "Who're you?"

"Wayne." He suddenly smiled, which made him look almost pleasant except for a large gap where one of his front teeth should have been. He took a couple steps nearer and extended one of his big, meaty hands.

"It's okay, Vic," Erin said. She advanced and took his hand. "Thanks for coming, Wayne. You know the score?"

"Yeah. I gotta take you and the rest of your crew downtown. It's cool, I got a delivery to make on the Lower East Side. Got my truck thataway." He jerked his head in the direction of the exit.

"Let's go," she said. Wayne started walking and the rest of them followed, Vic steering the reluctant Stone by the elbow.

"Erin, who is this guy?" Vic asked in an undertone.

"Wayne," she replied quietly, as if that explained things.

"He said he works for Corky," Vic went on. "Is that who I think it is?"

"Probably."

Vic rolled his eyes. "This day just gets better and better. You just keep an eye on him."

Wayne led them out of the station to the parking lot. A big rig sat there, immense and impressive. It was painted dark, glossy green with red flames on the sides of the hood. The big man ambled to the cab.

"That's our ride?" Erin asked.

"Yep. This is the Beast." Wayne laid an affectionate hand on the truck. He grinned, like a horse breeder showing off a prize stallion. "Got a brand-new Detroit Diesel DD16 under the hood. Displaces fifteen-point-six liters, rocks six hundred horses at eighteen hundred RPM."

"What kind of torque do you get?" Vic asked, interested in spite of himself. He liked engines.

"Two thousand and fifty pound-feet at nine seventy-five RPM," Wayne said proudly. "You name it, the Beast can pull it. This baby can yank the fillings right outta your teeth."

"That might be a little overkill for us," Erin said. But she looked doubtfully at the cab. There was no way he'd be able to make room for all of them up there.

Wayne followed her look. "Sorry, but only one of you gets to ride up front. I got some space in back. I'm not fully loaded for this trip. It'll be a little bumpy, but it ain't a long run down to the Big Apple. Good thing I'm not carrying meat this trip."

"Why's that?" she asked.

"Cause then it'd be a refrigerator trailer," Wayne said and guffawed. "Have to thaw you out once we got there."

"What's the load today?" Erin asked.

Wayne's smile compressed into a thin line. "Candy bars," he said in a flat voice.

"Candy bars," Erin repeated.

"Gotta keep those vending machines stocked," Wayne said. "So, who's up front?"

"I'd like to volunteer," Stone said.

"Shut up," Vic told him. "You better go up front, Erin."

"How unusually chivalrous of you," she said.

"Nah, I just want to keep an eye on this asshole." Vic elbowed Stone, who stumbled sideways and gave him an indignant look.

"I'll be adding assault to your growing list of misconduct violations," Stone said.

"You know more about assault than I do," Vic growled. "If I assault you, you'll damn well know it. You'll be walking funny for a week."

"Lay off, Vic," Erin said. "You want to ride in back, I'm not going to argue. What about Rolf?"

"That Rolf?" Wayne asked, indicating the K-9.

"Yeah."

"He can ride with us," Wayne said. "Between the seats. I like dogs." He offered his hand to the Shepherd, who gave it a professional sniff.

The trucker opened the sliding door on the back of the semi-trailer, revealing an interior about two-thirds full of cardboard boxes. They were labeled with the logos of the Mars candy company.

"You going to be okay in here?" Erin asked.

"Hey, my first apartment in the big city was less comfy than this," Vic said. "Had less furniture, too. Go on, jackass. Up you go."

"It's not easy to climb with my hands chained together," Stone complained.

Vic shrugged. Then he put his hands under Stone's armpits and hoisted the other man like a sack of potatoes, depositing him in the truck's interior. Stone was big, but Vic hefted him without much apparent effort. He climbed up after the prisoner.

"Don't let him get away with anything," Erin said quietly. "We won't be able to help you back there. Maybe I should keep your gun."

It was a sensible precaution. Even if Stone's hands had been free, Vic could easily overpower him in an unarmed fight. But if the prisoner got his hands on Vic's pistol, there could be trouble.

It was the same reasoning that led cops to lock up their guns before going into lockup areas or interrogation rooms.

"Yeah, sure," Vic said. "Why not?" He unbuckled his Sig-Sauer automatic from his waist, then bent down and took out his backup ankle piece and handed both pistols to Erin.

Wayne watched the whole thing, still smiling. "You guys good?" he asked. "Don't mean to be pushy, but I got a schedule to keep."

Vic gave him a thumbs-up. Wayne hopped up on the trailer with surprising agility for a guy his size, grabbed the pull-strap on the bottom of the trailer door, and slammed it shut, leaving Vic and Stone locked inside. Then Wayne, Erin, and Rolf got into the cab. Wayne turned the ignition. The Beast's engine roared to life and the big rig started rolling.

"So, you know Corky?" Erin asked.

"Everybody knows Corky," Wayne said. "He didn't mention you guys was cops."

"Must've slipped his mind," she said. "Forget about it."

"Nah, he said you was associated with Cars," Wayne persisted. "And Corky ain't stupid. He pretends he's not payin' attention, but he hears everything and he don't forget nothin.'"

"Ask around," she said. "Any of Corky's people can tell you anything you need to know about me."

Wayne nodded, satisfied. "Nice dog you got there. He a cop, too?"

"Yeah, he's a K-9."

"Narc dog?"

"No, he does search-and-rescue, suspect apprehension, and explosives sniffing."

"I gotta get me a dog," Wayne said. "A lot of the guys who do long-haul gigs got one. Makes it less lonesome on the road. What breed you recommend?"

"German Shepherd," she said, not needing to think about it.

"I'll look into it," he said. "You know anybody gots a puppy they wanna get rid of?"

Erin smiled. That was how Corky and Carlyle's world worked. It was all networking, going off people you knew. Even when it came to getting a new dog. "I'll ask around," she said. "But Rolf came all the way from Germany. I think you might want something more local, and maybe a little less expensive."

"How much he run you?"

"The Department paid, but it was a few grand."

He whistled, impressed.

They drove for a few minutes in silence. Wayne, an experienced truck driver, knew exactly what he was doing behind the wheel. He handled the Beast with an easy grace, coaxing the truck onto the freeway as easily as if it had been a station wagon.

"You didn't ask why a couple of cops needed a lift to Manhattan with a guy in cuffs," Erin said at last.

"Ain't my business," Wayne said. "I don't need to know nothin.'"

Erin found his answer weirdly refreshing. She was sick and tired of her activities being watched by everyone. At least when you were dealing with criminals, they didn't tend to be nosy. Too much curiosity was a sign a guy might be working for the police. Wayne wanted her to know he was a stand-up guy who kept his nose in his own business. Even though she *was* the police.

She had the rest of the drive home to wonder why that made her feel better about the guy who was helping her out.

Chapter 13

The drive was going smoothly, except for Wayne's fondness for country-western music. Erin was more of a pop rock girl, though she wouldn't admit to liking some of the singers she secretly enjoyed. She endured it for as long as she could. Then, right at the New York state line, she couldn't resist anymore.

"Hey, Wayne?" she said.

"Yeah?"

"You ever heard what happens when you play a country-western song backwards?"

"Yeah, I heard that one," he said. "You get your house back, you get your truck back, your wife comes home, your dog comes back to life, and they let you out of jail."

"You're not laughing."

"It's not funny." Then he glanced in his rearview mirror. "Ah, crap."

"What?" Erin checked the mirror on her side. She saw flashing lights framing the sleek, midnight-blue shape of a New York State Patrol cruiser. It was coming up on their tail, clearly targeting the Beast.

"Registration in the glove box?" she asked.

Wayne hesitated. "Yeah, but be careful when you open it," he said. Then, with a resigned sigh, he pulled over to the shoulder and slowed to a stop.

Erin gingerly popped the catch on the glove compartment and saw why Wayne was concerned. A gigantic revolver, a Smith & Wesson .44, lay there, black and menacing, like a waiting rattlesnake.

"Don't suppose you've got a permit for that?" she asked.

"I got a record," Wayne said, which answered the question. A convicted felon was about as likely to obtain a legal permit for a handgun in New York as Erin was to find a winning lottery ticket in the gutter.

The State Patrol car pulled over behind them. The trooper got out, squared his broad-brimmed hat on his head, and started toward them.

Now Erin had a dilemma, and she had until the other cop got to the cab to decide what to do. She was riding in a truck with an ex-con with an illegal firearm and God only knew what in the trailer, along with her fellow detective and a man in handcuffs. If she took the high road, Wayne would go to jail and Erin would have some explaining to do. She'd also have a big problem with Corky and the O'Malleys. But if she covered for Wayne, she'd gain points with the O'Malleys and maybe avoid other legal entanglements.

The only downside was, she'd have to turn a blind eye to at least one obvious crime.

The trooper was only a few feet away now. The man adjusted his belt, keeping one hand casually in the vicinity of his sidearm. The New York State Police carried Glock 37s, the .45-caliber big brother of Erin's own Glock 19. Those could blow a sizable hole in just about anything.

"If he asks anything awkward, I got this," she said to Wayne.

He nodded, keeping his hands above the steering wheel. This obviously wasn't his first time being pulled over.

The trooper rapped on the door with his knuckles and motioned for Wayne to roll down the window. The big guy obeyed.

"Evening, Trooper," Wayne said.

"You know why I pulled you over, sir?" the trooper asked.

Wayne shrugged. "Dunno, sir. I'm not pulling too much weight, I know that for sure. My tags are up to date."

"What're you carrying?"

"Candy bars."

"Got the manifest there?"

"Sure thing, man." Wayne took out a packet of papers and passed it through the window.

"License and registration," the trooper added.

Erin handed it over to Wayne, who gave it to the trooper. She carefully closed the glove compartment, leaving the .44 magnum inside.

There was a pause while the trooper scanned the documents. "Wayne McClernand," he said. "Anything I ought to know about you, Wayne?"

Wayne shrugged again. "What's there to say?"

"If I open up the back, am I going to find anything that's not on this?" the trooper asked, pointing to the manifest.

"Dunno why you'd think that," Wayne said.

"Heard there might be a load of smokes coming through here," the trooper said. "To get around state taxes. You wouldn't have any cartons of cigs in there, Wayne, that didn't make it onto the manifest, now would you?"

Wayne shrugged again. "Hey, I just pull the freight. I don't load the boxes. Says on the manifest it's candy, I don't argue, and I don't open the boxes. I'm just doin' my job, man."

"And I'm doing mine," the trooper said. "Please step out of the vehicle. You too, ma'am."

"Excuse me, sir," Erin said.

"I said, out of the vehicle, please," the trooper repeated. He stepped back half a pace. Something about her and Wayne triggered his instincts. He was ready for trouble.

"No problem, man," Wayne said. He opened his door and jumped heavily down to the pavement. He was several inches taller and probably sixty pounds heavier than the trooper, who wasn't a little guy.

"Whoa, what you got in there?" the trooper said. He'd caught sight of Rolf through the open door.

"Police K-9, sir," Erin said. "I'm a detective with the NYPD."

Whatever the trooper had been expecting, it wasn't that. He blinked. "Come again?"

"Detective O'Reilly," she said. "NYPD Major Crimes. I've got my ID here. I'm going to get it out."

"Slow and easy," the trooper said. His hand was now on his Glock.

Wayne, standing next to the Beast's idling engine, said nothing. He seemed more curious than apprehensive now.

Erin told Rolf, "*Bleib.*"

Rolf stayed put. He cocked his head at the state trooper.

Erin worked her way past her dog to the driver's side so she wouldn't be out of the trooper's line of sight and climbed out of the cab. She produced her shield and showed it to the trooper. He bent forward to examine it.

"You're off the reservation a little, Detective," he said.

"On my way home now," she said.

He motioned her to move away from the truck, out of earshot of Wayne. "You stay put, big guy," he told Wayne.

"Not goin' anywhere, man," Wayne said.

"What's the story, O'Reilly?" the trooper demanded in a low voice. "I'm working a tip on a cigarette-smuggling operation here. Now I run into a New York City cop? Why wasn't I told you guys were in on this?"

Erin shrugged. "I'm working a Major Crimes case on the organization behind the smuggling," she said. "This guy's helping me with my investigation." Both those things were technically true, although they referred to two completely separate cases. He didn't need to know that.

"So he does have contraband in back," the trooper said.

"I haven't checked the boxes myself," she said. "But yeah, probably."

"I'm supposed to bring the trucker in," the trooper said. "My CO thinks we can flip him and maybe get the guy behind it."

"The trucker's nobody," she said. "Just an ex-con they've got as a mule. And I've already got on the inside with him. You arrest him, it's going to screw up my investigation."

The trooper pushed back his hat and scratched his head. "The Lieutenant's gonna be pissed," he muttered.

"You're doing me a solid," she said. "What's your name, Trooper?"

"Owen Dunbar."

"I won't forget this, Dunbar." She offered her hand.

He looked at her for a moment, then shook. "I hope I don't regret this," he said.

Dunbar walked back to the truck with Erin. "Drive carefully," he said, handing Wayne his paperwork. "Ma'am," he added, tipping his hat slightly to Erin before heading back to his cruiser. The dark, predatory silhouette of the patrol car glided onto the highway and lost itself in the southbound traffic.

"Thanks," Wayne said to Erin. "How'd you manage that?"

"Forget about it," she said. "Can we get back to my city now?"

"Lady," he said, "after that, I'll take you anywhere you wanna go. Just name it."

The rest of the trip was as uneventful as a journey could be when you stuck a couple of cops, a K-9, and a murder suspect in a truck driven by a convicted felon. Erin used the time to think. Webb was right. Stone would lawyer up fast, with a high-powered legal team, and unless they had hard evidence, they wouldn't be able to hold him. But what evidence was there to find? They couldn't get the proof they needed without full access to the hotel room, and for that they needed a warrant, which they couldn't get without more evidence. It was a classic catch-22.

Except it wasn't. There was one way to get unfiltered access to a room. Erin was astonished she hadn't thought of it sooner. It was obvious, really. Now she just needed to get back to Manhattan.

* * *

"What the hell was that all about?" Vic asked when Wayne opened the trailer and spilled him and Stone onto the pavement.

"Tell you in a minute," Erin said.

"Where are we, anyway?" he asked.

She cocked her head. He turned and found himself staring at the old brick façade of the Eightball station house.

"Dropped us right at the front door," he said. "Now that's service."

"Yeah," Wayne said. "Maybe I should get me a taxi instead." He smiled, showing the gap in his teeth. "Nah, I love the Beast too much. Catch you later, O'Reilly. I got deliveries to make."

He offered a hand. Erin, surprised, shook. Her slender hand disappeared into his gigantic paw. Wayne's smile widened into a grin.

"Say, after I unload, I got some time," he said. "If you wanna grab a drink or something."

Erin returned the smile. "You know the Barley Corner?"

"Of course. Wanna meet me there?"

"Why don't you drop by there," she said. "Ask around. They'll tell you everything you need to know about me."

Wayne's smile faltered a little as he realized he might have stepped in something he didn't want any part of. He let go of her hand. Then he closed the trailer and walked back to the Beast's cab. He climbed in and drove away.

"I'd like my telephone call now," Stone said. "And after that, I will obviously want the benefit of legal counsel."

"That's your right," Erin said. Then, to Vic, "Let's book him."

"Then maybe we can get something to eat?" Vic suggested. They'd burned a good couple of hours with their jaunt to and from Connecticut and it was after seven.

She shook her head. "We've got work to do."

"All work and no play?" Stone said. "That's not healthy, Miss O'Reilly."

"Neither is your style of play," she shot back.

They got Stone booked. Then they had to follow the law and give him access to a phone. Predictably, he called a lawyer up in Boston. It was a very short conversation.

After that they moved Stone into a holding cell. Erin made sure to walk him past Caldwell's cell so the two men could get a quick look at each other. When dealing with a conspiracy, it was almost always a good idea to let the suspects know their collaborators were also in custody, but to keep them separated. They'd have the chance to sit and wonder what their counterparts were telling the police, and what kind of deal they might be making. Erin had seen crooks turn on each other in those circumstances, confessing when the DA hadn't had anywhere near enough evidence for a conviction.

Once they had Stone safely stowed, Erin, Vic, and Rolf got on the elevator up to Major Crimes.

"That's gotta be a new one," Vic said.

"What?" Erin asked.

"Getting a Mob guy to drop off a couple police hitchhikers with a prisoner on the front steps of their precinct house."

"You think Wayne's mobbed up?" Erin asked with feigned innocence.

Vic gave her a look. "I may not be a fancy-pants Detective Second Grade like some of the people on this elevator, but I've got eyes and a brain. I saw the jailhouse tats on that guy. And if those boxes only had Snickers bars in them, I'll field-strip my sidearm and eat it one piece at a time."

"Now that I'd like to see," she said. Then she lowered her voice to a whisper. "No, you're right. This is helping me out with that other thing."

His jaw tightened. "Yeah, I figured. Way to kill two birds with one stone. Speaking of Stone..."

"We need evidence," she said. "Or he's going to walk."

"Okay. But the body was underwater for hours. CSU didn't pull any fibers or DNA off her. We know Stone took her to dinner, but that's not against the law. We got no case, Erin."

"Not yet," she said. "According to Webb, we've got maybe three hours before Stone's lawyers get here."

"We're gonna build a murder case in three hours," Vic said doubtfully. "How you plan on doing that?"

The elevator arrived at Major Crimes. There was Webb, as promised, at his desk. He had a Styrofoam takeout box and coffee cup in front of him and a sour look on his face.

"You're back," he said. "And the lawyers?"

"On their way," Erin said.

"I'll break out the ESU gear," Vic said. "If we barricade the front door, we should be able to hold them off for a while. It'll be just like *Assault on Precinct 13*. I love that movie."

"Not funny, Neshenko. I assume you have a plan?"

"Don't look at me, boss," Vic said. "I just work here."

"I have an idea," Erin said. "The first thing I need is the victim's clothes."

"They're down in Evidence," Webb said. "Where are you going with this?"

"Back to the hotel," she said. "Rolf and I have some searching to do."

"You don't have a warrant," he reminded her.

"All I need is permission."

"You think you'll get it?"

"Yes, sir, I do."

He stood up. "This I have to see. I'm coming along."

"Me, too," Vic said.

"No, you're staying here," Webb said.

"Why? What'd I do?" Vic asked indignantly.

"Someone needs to, how did you say it, hold off the lawyers," Webb said. "Preferably without resorting to tear gas and riot gear."

"What do you want me to use?" he shot back. "Strong language?"

"I want you to call me and then stall," Webb said. "Go by the book, but use every page you can. If you get stumped, call Kira Jones. She knows every NYPD procedure."

"You want me to get the bastards tangled up in our bureaucracy?" Vic shrugged. "Okay, sir, but I think tear gas might be more humane."

"We're wasting time," Webb said. "Let's go, O'Reilly."

"Look on the bright side, Vic," Erin said on her way out. "Looks like you get dinner after all."

Chapter 14

Armed with a paper bag containing a pair of underwear worn by the late Sarah Devers, Erin set off for the InterContinental. Webb was in the passenger seat, Rolf in his compartment. The Lieutenant fingered an unlit cigarette and brooded. The K-9 panted excitedly.

"So what's your plan?" Webb asked.

"You're the ranking officer," she said.

"I'm aware of that, O'Reilly. And as such, I'm ordering you to tell me what you want to do here."

"As ranking officer, sir, you'd obviously be the one who'd request access to information from the hotel."

Webb waited and said nothing.

"So I think it'd be good for you to do just that."

"While you're doing... what, exactly?"

"Getting a room for the night."

He blinked. Then he actually laughed. "A particular room, I assume. 503, maybe?"

"Exactly, sir. That'll give me all the access I need."

"While I'm distracting anyone who might recognize you as a cop and worry about what you might be up to," Webb said.

"All perfectly legal, of course. But there's a few problems. What if they've already rented out that room?"

"Stone checked out a day early," she said. "But he left after the usual checkout time. I'm guessing they haven't had long to get it ready for the next occupant."

"If they've cleaned the room, you may not find what you're looking for," he went on. "And if they haven't, they won't let you have it."

"Let me handle it, sir."

"By bribing hotel staff?"

"I plan to encourage their civic impulses," she said with a straight face. "I have a question for you, sir."

"Shoot."

"If this works, can I expense the room to the NYPD?"

"I don't see why not. And list any payoffs to the staff as payments to unnamed confidential informants. It's only bribery if *they* pay *us*."

* * *

At the hotel, Erin and Rolf split off from Webb. The Lieutenant led the way.

"Give me about a minute," he said.

Erin obediently hung around outside the front door, sneaking a quick glance inside. She saw him approach Mr. Feldspar and start talking to him. She waited, trusting her commanding officer. Sure enough, after a moment, the two men walked away from the front desk and disappeared into the manager's office.

Erin sauntered in with Rolf, trying to appear nonchalant. She'd moved her Glock to the small of her back under her blouse, where it wouldn't be visible to a casual search, and had pocketed her shield. Rolf wasn't wearing his K-9 vest. Hopefully they wouldn't be too conspicuous.

The clean-cut young man behind the counter gave her a bright, friendly smile. "Good evening, ma'am. How can I help you?"

Erin gave him her best, warmest smile in return. "Hi! I just got in, a last-minute business thing. I didn't have time to make a reservation. Can you help me out?"

"Sure thing, ma'am. I know, that can be a real hassle. Name?"

"Erin O'Reilly."

"How many guests? Just you?"

"And this guy," she said, twitching Rolf's leash.

The man's face fell. "Ma'am, I'm sorry, but there's a weight limit on pets of twenty-five pounds."

"Oh, he's not a pet," Erin said. She leaned forward and lowered her voice. "Service dogs aren't prohibited, are they?"

"Of course not, ma'am. I'll just need to see his certification."

Erin cursed inwardly. She made a show of pulling out her wallet and searching for something she knew damned well wasn't there. Then she decided the hell with it. She palmed her shield and flashed it to him.

"I'm undercover with the NYPD," she whispered. "He's a K-9. We're working a big bust."

"There aren't drugs in the hotel, are there?" he whispered back, looking both alarmed and excited.

"No, nothing like that," she assured him. "But I need to keep this on the down-low. I can't discuss it, but can you make an exception to your policy?"

He nodded. "Yeah, I'd say he looks like he's about twenty-five pounds, ma'am." He didn't quite wink or lay a finger alongside his nose, but his eyes twinkled.

Rolf, who weighed every ounce of ninety pounds, was unimpressed.

"I'm afraid I do have to charge you the extra two-fifty for him," he said. "Sorry, ma'am."

"*Two hundred fifty dollars?*" Erin hissed, appalled.

"Yes, ma'am. It's the rules."

"Okay, whatever," she said, glad she'd cleared it with Webb for departmental reimbursement. "One other thing. Can I request a specific room?"

"Certainly, ma'am, if it's available."

"I'd like 503, please."

"Just a second." He worked his computer. "Oh, I'm sorry, ma'am."

"It hasn't been rented out, has it?" she asked.

"No, but it was just recently vacated and hasn't been changed over yet. Housekeeping will get right on it, but it's just not ready."

"Oh, that's okay," she said. "I'm not going to be sleeping just yet. Tell you what, Stu," she said, looking at his nametag. "I'll just go on up there and you can send housekeeping up. When they arrive, I'll get out of their hair."

"But ma'am, 504 is right across the hall and it's vacant," Stu said. "It's no hassle, really."

She tried to up the wattage on her smile a little bit more. "I have some memories of 503. It'd mean a lot to me." She put a hand on the counter and tapped her finger, drawing his attention to the twenty-dollar bill under her hand.

Stu nodded. "Absolutely, ma'am. I'll make sure they get right on it."

*   *   *

Erin slid the keycard into its slot and opened the door to Room 503. There was no reason to believe anyone else was there, but she still cleared the bedroom and bathroom with as much care as if she was entering a drug den or gang headquarters. The fact that she'd been ambushed in her own apartment less than two weeks earlier was very much on her mind. She and Rolf checked their corners, opened the closet, and looked under the bed.

Nobody was there, of course. Erin relaxed and holstered her Glock. Then she got to work. She opened the paper bag, extracted the scrap of satin inside, and presented it to Rolf.

"*Such!*" she ordered.

Rolf sniffed at the undergarment. Then he stood in the middle of the room for a few moments, snuffling the air and turning around. His tail wagged uncertainly.

It wasn't that he couldn't smell Sarah Devers, Erin knew. It was that Sarah had been in the room and wasn't there anymore. She'd come and gone and probably wandered around a little. Rolf was trying to pick up the freshest scent.

He trotted into the bathroom and stood in front of the toilet. He got in close to the porcelain and inhaled, nostrils twitching.

Erin knelt beside the K-9 and peered at the toilet. She didn't see anything at first, but she caught a faint acidic tang on the air. Then she took a breath and leaned over the bowl, holding her hair back by its ponytail so it wouldn't fall in the water. She saw what she'd thought she might find. Little spots of something that looked and smelled like bile were splashed up under the rim of the toilet bowl.

"Thank God for slow housekeeping," Erin muttered. Rolf was telling her Sarah had been in here and had probably thrown up, likely as a result of being drugged or drinking too much. CSU could get DNA off the toilet, and if they were lucky, traces of Rohypnol. That would prove she'd been drugged before leaving Stone's room.

Rolf wasn't finished. The Shepherd's feet danced impatiently. He tugged on his leash. Erin stood up and followed her dog out into the bedroom. The bed was rumpled and unmade, which made sense. Stu shouldn't have let her have this room in its current state, cop or no cop, tip or no tip. But she had no complaints. He was helping her preserve evidence.

Rolf nosed his way across the carpet. Erin saw little bits of discoloration, probably from residual vomit. Then the Shepherd abruptly stood on his hind legs and put his paws on the bed. He thrust under one of the pillows with his snout. Then he pulled back and looked at Erin, cocking his head.

"It's okay, kiddo," she said, scratching his ears. "I know she's not here."

She pulled on a pair of disposable gloves and picked up the pillow Rolf had sniffed at. Under it, next to the headboard, she saw a glint of color against the white sheets. She bent closer and saw a broken piece of fingernail.

"Gotcha," she said. She saw a faint gouge in the wood of the headboard near the nail fragment. She also smelled more hints of vomit on the sheets.

"Sarah came in and shared a drink with Stone," Erin told Rolf, who watched her attentively. He liked when Erin talked to him.

"But there was more in the drink than booze," she went on. "She got dizzy, but she didn't completely pass out. He tried to get at her on the bed, but she still had a little fight in her. She struggled and broke a fingernail. Then she started gagging. That probably made him let go of her. Even a rapist won't try to kiss someone who's puking. She made it into the bathroom. I think she passed out in there. He pulled her out onto the bedroom floor. She was unconscious and unresponsive. He tried to do CPR, but it was too late. She died right there."

Erin pointed to the patch of carpet Rolf had investigated. Rolf followed her finger with his eyes and wagged his tail. He'd already checked that spot. He was waiting for further instructions.

"So now Stone had a body to get rid of," she said. "He needed hotel security to do that. Lucky for him, the security chief was a corrupt ex-cop who could be bought. Caldwell doctored the elevator cameras and cut power to the third floor. Then he carried the body down and stashed it. No, that doesn't play. How did he get the body out? He wouldn't have risked running into someone in the hallway or on the elevator. He had to have hidden it somehow."

She looked around the room, seeking inspiration, and came up with nothing.

"What am I missing?" she asked her dog.

Rolf wagged his tail. He had complete faith in her.

There was a knock on the door. "Housekeeping!" a female voice called in accented English.

Erin cursed quietly. Stu had been a little too efficient. She went to the door and opened it to reveal Rosa Hernandez with her cleaning cart.

"I am so sorry," Rosa said. "I clean the room quickly. Maybe you want to go and come back? Twenty, thirty minutes."

"No, that's okay," Erin said. "Rosa, I need you to do something for me."

The maid did a double-take at the sound of her own name. Then recognition dawned in her eyes. "You were here with the police," she said.

"I still am," Erin said. "Can you help me?"

"I do not want trouble," Rosa said, looking nervously around.

"You're not in any trouble. But there's important evidence in this room. You can't clean it yet." Then her eyes went past Rosa to the cart. It had shelves in the middle, on which fresh towels and rolls of toilet paper were piled. But on either end were big yellow plastic bags. Were they big enough?

"Rosa," Erin said. "You were working in the morning, when you found the woman in the water. When did you come to work?"

"Eight o' clock," she said. "I work twelve hours, eight until eight."

"Who did you replace?"

"I do not understand."

"Who worked the night shift before you?"

"Josefina."

"What's Josefina's last name?"

Rosa shook her head. "I want no one to be in trouble."

Erin put a hand on Rosa's shoulder. The Latina was trembling. "Are you worried Josefina will get in trouble? Be deported, maybe? Is she in this country illegally?"

Rosa hesitated. Then, hearing only compassion in Erin's voice, she nodded.

"Does anyone who works at the hotel know that about her?" Erin asked.

Rosa nodded again. "Mr. Caldwell," she said. "And Mr. Feldspar. They know about... all of us. It is cheaper for them to hire us. We work for less money."

"I need to talk with her," Erin said. "If she cooperates with us, I promise, she won't be deported."

"Her name is Josefina Perez."

"Thank you. Now please, Rosa, don't touch anything in this room. It's very important."

Rosa nodded unhappily. She stood there in the hallway, clutching one of her elbows. She was clearly frightened. "They will know," she said quietly.

"What? Who will know?" Erin asked sharply.

Rosa flinched. "They see everything, they know everything that happens here. I will lose my job."

"Feldspar and Caldwell?"

But Rosa just clamped her lips together and shook her head, refusing to say more.

Erin had a sudden thought, remembering what Polk had said in his interrogation. She turned away from the housekeeper and looked at the bedroom. She wasn't looking at the furniture now. She was looking for places to hide something. Something very small.

"There'll be one over the bed," she said softly. "And maybe in the bathroom."

She walked to the bed and looked up. A ceiling fan and light fixture hung there. The rest of the ceiling was featureless white plaster. She carefully put a foot on the bedframe and another on the headboard to avoid trampling any evidence on the sheets. Rolf stood at the base of the bed and looked curiously up at her.

Erin peered at the fan. For a moment she didn't see it. Then she did; the tiny, shiny eye of a miniature camera lens.

"Gotcha," she said again. "You son of a bitch."

That camera changed everything. Erin hauled out her phone and dialed Webb.

"You're in?" Webb asked.

"I'm in," she confirmed. "Sir, where are you?"

"I just grabbed a hot dog off a street cart. I'm half a block down the way."

"Can you get back here?"

"You've got something?" He suddenly sounded more energized.

"I know how Stone did it," she said. "And I know who helped him. Bring Feldspar up with you."

"You sure you want him in on this?"

"I'm sure. Don't let him leave."

Chapter 15

"Here we are, O'Reilly," Webb said. He was standing half a step behind Feldspar in room 503's doorway, in a posture Erin recognized. He was making sure the other man didn't make a run for it. Feldspar looked uncomfortable and nervous, sweating through the collar of his expensive suit.

"I'd be happy to assist with anything the New York Police Department needs," Feldspar said. "But I do have some urgent business to attend to. I can put you in touch with the assistant manager if you'd like."

"He's not kidding about the urgent business," Webb said. "He was trying to sneak out the back when I found him."

"I wasn't sneaking anywhere," Feldspar protested. "My car is parked out back."

"Hurrying, then," Webb amended.

"C'mon in," Erin said. "We need to talk, Mr. Feldspar."

The manager glanced over his shoulder. Webb wasn't a physically imposing man. But middle-aged, balding, and overweight as he was, he could still project authority when he wanted to. Feldspar swallowed and entered the room. Webb followed him in, closing the door behind him and standing in front of it.

"I'm going to tell you what happened in this room," Erin said. "There was a charity dinner a couple nights ago in the ballroom downstairs. One of the attendees was a guy named Wendell J. Stone."

"The third," Webb added with a slight smile.

"He's a rich guy, from a powerful family up in Boston," she went on. "He's used to being able to get what he wants. Usually he uses his money or his connections, but he's not above a little pharmaceutical assistance. He wanted a pretty girl on his arm at dinner, and in his bed after."

"Please, ma'am," Feldspar said. "You don't have to go into all that—"

"He knew about a modeling agency called Ethereal Angels," she cut him off. "They would provide an escort for dinner. That's often understood to be code for a call girl, but in this case, the wires must have gotten crossed. They didn't loan him a hooker for the evening. They hired out an innocent modelnamed Sarah Devers.

"It's possible he requested someone more innocent," Erin allowed. "Maybe he liked the idea of seducing her. In any case, after dinner, he invited her up to his room for a drink. Then he tried to put the moves on her. But she wasn't having any of it. There was a struggle. A gentleman would've given up and let her go. But not Stone. He was going to get what he'd paid for.

"He had the drugs with him. He'd already suspected he might have to take steps. It wasn't the first time he'd done it. So he apologized, said he wouldn't try anything else, gave her a drink to calm her down. But the drink had a little something extra in it.

"Rohypnol can be tricky to dose someone with. Get the amount wrong and it can really mess with you. And it can interact with alcohol. Sarah got sick. She threw up there on the bed, then stumbled into the bathroom and passed out. Stone wasn't too scared yet. This was nothing he couldn't handle. Until he realized she wasn't breathing."

Erin paused and looked closely at Feldspar. He was sweating more visibly and seemed to have tied his necktie too tightly. He was working at it with his fingers, trying to loosen his collar.

"I'll give Stone this," she said. "He didn't want Sarah to die. But all he had to go on was some old CPR training. He should've called 911. That might have saved her life, if the paramedics had gotten here fast enough."

She met Feldspar's eye as he tried to look away. "There was a lot of that going on. More than one person could have saved her life."

"I don't know what you mean," he said.

Erin walked over to the bed. For the second time, she jumped up on the mattress. She pulled on a new plastic glove from the roll in her pocket, reached up, and yanked on the ceiling fan. The miniature camera came loose in her hand. It trailed a thin power cable and hung there like a discarded fishing lure.

"What's that?" Feldspar asked, his voice a faint croak.

"Spy camera," she said. "Illegal, of course."

The manager cleared his throat. "You don't have a search warrant," he said.

"I'm a paying customer of the hotel," she said. "I'm on the books downstairs. I discovered an illegal surveillance device in my room, and I'm reporting it to the proper authorities. Lieutenant Webb?"

"Duly noted," Webb said. "The NYPD is prepared to take your statement, Detective O'Reilly. I'll call it in."

"Our CSU guys are really good," Erin said. "Don't worry, Mr. Feldspar. They should be able to figure out where this camera's signal goes. We'll know within the next couple of hours who's been spying on your hotel's guests."

"Thank you," he said. "If that's all, I should really report this to the board of directors." He turned toward the door.

"You're not going anywhere until we clear this up, sir," Webb said. "You see, we have to assume the perpetrator is a hotel employee. For all we know, it might be you."

Feldspar looked from Webb to Erin and back again. He licked his lips nervously. "Don't be ridiculous," he said.

"You saw it happen," Erin said quietly. "You knew who killed Sarah the whole time. Did you watch while it was happening?"

Erin had a good eye for human weakness. After twelve years wearing a shield, she could usually tell when a perp was about to crack. She saw Feldspar crumble.

He nodded miserably. "Yes. I watched. He put her on the bed and they... she... oh God. I didn't do anything. It wasn't me!"

"No, you didn't do anything," Erin said with quiet contempt. "You just watched a girl die. Because that's what you do, Nick. You watch."

"I can't help it," he said. "I've tried to stop. I can't. It's like a drug. You don't understand. And what was the harm? No one ever knew about it. I didn't show the tapes to anyone."

"There's tapes?" Webb asked. "Where?"

"My office. On a thumb drive."

Webb had his phone out almost before Feldspar finished the sentence, calling in reinforcements. "This is Webb, Major Crimes, shield six-four-four-two. I need two units to the InterContinental Hotel, manager's office. They are to secure the office. No one goes in, nothing comes out. And I need a CSU team with someone who can do data retrieval, forthwith."

While Webb was on the phone, Erin focused on Feldspar. The manager was actually in tears.

"Did you get the whole thing on film?" she asked.

He nodded.

"How did it happen?"

"Like you said," he whispered. "After a couple of minutes, Mr. Stone stopped pounding on her chest. Then he made a call, to the security desk I assume. Mr. Caldwell met him in the hallway. I don't know what they did out there."

"You only have hidden cameras in the rooms," she said.

"That's right. Then they came into the room and looked at... at her. Then Mr. Caldwell made a phone call. A few minutes later, Josefina came in. He talked to her for a little while."

"What did they say?"

"I don't know. The cameras don't have audio. Just images."

Erin nodded. "Go on."

"Caldwell and Josefina took the... the body to the door. They took her outside. Josefina came back in after about ten minutes. She washed the bathroom and put some cleaner on the carpet and the sheets. Then she left."

"She didn't do a very good job," Webb observed. He'd gotten off the phone and was listening with interest.

"No," Erin said, "she didn't. She should've taken the dirty sheets away and replaced them. It's almost like she wanted evidence left behind."

"I need to talk to Josefina," Webb said. "Obviously."

"What then?" Erin asked Feldspar.

"That was it," he said. "Mr. Caldwell came back to the room and spoke with Mr. Stone in the doorway. Mr. Stone gave him something. Money, I think. Then Mr. Stone went to bed."

"He just went to sleep," Webb said, shaking his head. "After overdosing a girl right there in the room. Unbelievable."

"And you didn't tell us," Erin said.

"I thought... what difference did it make?" Feldspar said. "I couldn't help her. And I thought... I thought no one would see her again. Young women disappear in this city all the time. People would think she'd just run away or something. It might be better for her... for her family. To have hope. But then Rosa found her in the fish tank."

"Josefina and Caldwell were supposed to make the body disappear," Erin said. "But it didn't happen that way. I wonder why. And I wonder whether you really believe that line of bullshit you just gave us."

"What could I do?" he protested. "What would I say? That I'd been spying on hotel guests? I'd lose my job and go to jail."

"And now that's happening anyway," Erin said, taking out her handcuffs.

"Please!" he begged. "I told you everything!"

"You left us chasing our tails for days," she said. "You tried to weasel out of everything. The only reason you're talking now is because we already found you out and you've got nothing left to lose. You're pathetic. Nicholas Feldspar, you're under arrest for violation of the Sexually Violent Predator Law for placing unlawful surveillance equipment in a bedroom for the purpose of sexual gratification. We're also taking you in as an accessory after the fact for the murder of Sarah Devers. You have the right to remain silent. Anything you say can and will be used against you in a court of law..."

Erin had to talk louder as she continued reading the Miranda warning, because the hapless manager had dissolved into sobs. She had to pull his hands away from his face in order to get the cuffs on him.

*   *   *

Webb's phone rang while he, Erin, and Rolf were in the elevator with Feldspar. Erin saw Vic's name on the screen as her commanding officer brought the phone to his ear.

"Talk to me, Neshenko," he said.

They were standing close enough that Erin could faintly hear Vic's reply.

"Sir, you better get back here right now."

"What's happening?" Webb asked sharply.

"Lawyers."

"I thought we had more time," Webb said. "How'd they get down from Boston so fast?"

"He must have a local firm on retainer. What do you want me to do?"

"Don't let Stone out of the building. Keep him in holding as long as you can, then move him to interrogation with his lawyers. Drag your feet every step of the way. Filibuster. We're coming."

Webb hung up and sighed.

"What's the big deal, sir?" Erin asked. "We can hold him overnight if we want to."

"Not if the Captain tells us to release him."

"Why the hell would Holliday do that? He'll have our back."

"If the PC orders him to, he won't have a choice."

The elevator arrived at the ground floor. A pair of uniforms were waiting in the lobby.

"Sir," one of them said. "We've got the office secured. CSU's on the way."

"Good," Webb said. He thought for a moment. "O'Reilly, you better stay here. Get the film, then get back to the Eightball as fast as you can. I'll buy you some time."

"Just a second, sir," Erin said. She turned to Feldspar. "Listen to me. You want to make the murder accessory charges disappear?"

Feldspar lifted his head a little. "How?"

"Give us the correct thumb drive. Cooperate. Help us get the guy who killed Sarah. We'll find the film anyway, sooner or later. If you make it hard for us, it'll be worse for you."

Feldspar was completely defeated. He nodded obediently, almost pathetically eager to please. "Okay. Anything you need."

They took the manager into his soon-to-be-former office. Two more Patrol officers were there, keeping an eye on things.

"Left desk drawer," Feldspar said.

Erin pulled on her gloves and opened the drawer. "I don't see anything," she said. "Just office supplies. You yanking me around?"

"You need to pull the drawer all the way out," he said. "Look behind it."

She jiggled the drawer loose from its runners and pulled it free. A slim thumb drive with a USB port was stuck to the back with a piece of masking tape.

"This it?" she asked.

Feldspar nodded.

"Is there any encryption on it?"

He shook his head.

She curled her fingers around it and fished out an evidence bag.

"Let's go," Webb said.

* * *

They used the Charger's lights and siren as if someone's life depended on them getting back to the station as fast as humanly possible. Rolf, riding in his compartment, loved every minute of it. The only way the Shepherd would have enjoyed it more would have been for the windows to be rolled down so he could stick his head out.

Webb shot Vic a text message while Erin drove. "They're in the interrogation room," he reported. "He's been shuffling Stone around, dodging the lawyers, but he can't stall much longer." He extracted the drive from its bag, plugged it into her onboard computer, and spent the next few minutes looking through video files.

"Anything good, sir?" she asked.

"If you're planning on operating an illegal porn site, then yeah," he said. "Sergeant Brown ought to love this. Looks like the footage is sorted by floor. Okay, yeah. We want folder five, subfolder three, the clip stamped with the date of the crime. I'll just spot-check it... oh, this is excellent, O'Reilly."

Erin turned the corner and cruised up to the Eightball. She spun the wheel and laid rubber on the entrance ramp to the parking garage. "Here we are, sir."

"You go on in, O'Reilly. I'll grab our suspect and follow."

"Don't you want to be the one to nail Stone, sir?"

He smiled thinly and handed her the thumb drive. "This is your collar, O'Reilly. Besides, I'm too old to run up flights of stairs. I'll get started booking this guy."

"Copy that, sir." Erin realized Webb was giving her a simultaneous compliment and reward. He was saying he trusted her to bring the case home, and he knew she wanted to be the one to do it.

It didn't occur to her until she was halfway up the stairs that he might also be insulating himself against political blowback for busting the son of a powerful figure.

"That's why I'm never going to make Captain," she muttered to Rolf. "I don't play the game well enough."

Rolf, easily loping up the stairs beside her, wagged his tail enthusiastically. He liked games.

She didn't go directly to the interrogation room, in spite her hurry; she needed a computer for the thumb drive. They had a laptop up in Major Crimes, just in case a portable machine was ever needed. She scooped it up and glanced at Rolf.

"*Sitz,*" she told him. "*Bleib.*"

Those weren't his favorite commands, but he was good at them. Rolf sat and stayed, despite his confusion at being benched in the middle of all this excitement. Erin left him there and hurried back downstairs.

She found Vic in Interrogation Room One, together with Stone and a pair of men in suits too expensive to be anything but lawyers, or maybe mob bosses. Vic's face was red and he looked irritated.

"Detective," one of the lawyers was saying, "I understand your position, and you're only doing your job. But you're putting your department in a very serious position from a liability perspective. Now, if you had any real evidence—"

"Speak of the devil," Vic said, flashing Erin a look of mingled exasperation and relief. "Gentlemen, this is my colleague, Detective O'Reilly."

"Gentlemen," Erin repeated, reflecting on how Vic managed to make the word sound like an insult.

"Yes, you would be the officer in charge of abducting our client across state lines without a warrant," the other lawyer said. "Our client has been telling us all about you."

"In that case, he'll have told you I don't give up," Erin said, sliding into the chair next to Vic. She flipped open the laptop and turned it on.

"Unfortunately, yes," the first lawyer said. "You may have some personal liability as well as that pertaining to your department. I hope you're enjoying your temporary position of power, Detective. This may be your last day with the NYPD."

Erin let his words slide off her. She'd heard worse threats from more dangerous people. She was busy plugging in the thumb drive and opening the correct file. Vic, looking over her shoulder, saw what she was doing. When the top-down image of Room 503 appeared on screen, a slow, nasty smile spread over his face.

"Detective, are you even listening to me?" the lawyer demanded.

"I'm sorry for interrupting this interview," she said. "But I have something you and your client need to see. Before we get to that, just so I'm clear, does your client still claim he has no knowledge of the death of Sarah Devers, AKA Crystal Winters?"

"That is correct," the second lawyer said. "And whatever bluff you're planning, whatever fabricated evidence you may produce, I assure you, Detective, I'm not impressed."

In answer, Erin flipped the computer around to show the screen to the men on the other side of the table. Looking Stone straight in the eye, she started the video running.

The next minutes were five of the longest, quietest ones Erin had experienced in an interrogation room. The only sounds were the muffled whir of the laptop's fan and the breathing of the five people seated at the table.

"This recording was clearly illegally obtained," the first lawyer said, after they'd finished watching Sarah Devers die on the floor of the hotel bedroom. "It's inadmissible as evidence."

"That would be true," Erin admitted, "if it had been recorded by the NYPD, who would've needed a warrant for this sort of surveillance. But it wasn't. It's evidence in another criminal case. An employee of the hotel was in the habit of recording the guests. You're right, that's against the law, and he has also been arrested and will face the consequences of his actions. But he is cooperating with our investigation. The NYPD got this recording completely legitimately. You are, of course, free to employ a technical consultant to verify the authenticity of the recording." She smiled sweetly.

"That won't be necessary," Stone said.

"Mr. Stone," the second lawyer said warningly.

"No, Mr. Branch, I know what I'm saying," Stone said. His face had gone very pale while he'd watched the recording, but his voice was steady and his hands didn't tremble even a little. "It's rather late to persist in denials. It was an accident. No one was supposed to get hurt."

"You drugged her," Erin said, "with the intention of nonconsensual sexual intercourse."

"Otherwise known as rape," Vic added.

"She misrepresented herself," Stone said. "She promised something she had no intention of delivering. She violated our understanding. She's the guilty one here."

"What understanding was that?" Erin asked quietly.

"I engaged her services for the night," he said. "The *whole* night. With an implicit understanding of all that entails. She tried to renege on our deal."

"My client has no further comment," the first lawyer said in a last effort at damage control.

"Your client is paying your bills," Stone snapped. "Shut up. The grownups are talking."

The lawyer's mouth clamped shut, his lips pressed into a fine line. For once in Erin's life, she felt a little empathy for a defense attorney. He was watching his case disintegrate and his client wasn't letting him do his job.

Apparently, Stone was so used to getting away with things, he felt that he'd become immune. Maybe he genuinely didn't understand the gravity of what they were discussing. But mostly, Erin suspected, he wanted to justify himself. That was the trick of interrogations. A detective had to make herself into someone the perp wanted understanding from. If you could make that more important than, say, avoiding a prison sentence, you'd get your confession.

"And you wanted what you'd paid for," she said, ignoring the lawyers.

"That's how all businesses work," Stone said.

"What did you do with your drugs?" she asked. They hadn't found any in his belongings when they'd arrested him.

"I flushed the remainder down the commode. Again, I must insist, I didn't want her to die. I did my best to save her."

"Yeah, I know," Erin said. "You did everything you could, except for calling an ambulance, which might have actually kept her alive."

She stood up and flipped down the lid on the laptop. "Thanks for your time, counselors. Anything further you've got to say, you can save for the DA. It'll be up to him what degree of murder charges to bring. And Mr. Stone?"

He looked up at her in silence. His face remained pale but outwardly calm.

"A relationship isn't a business agreement. You can back out of it anytime you want. You had no right."

"We're taking your boy back to his nice comfy cell," Vic said to the lawyers. "Don't worry, I'm sure you can invoice him for his plea bargain."

Chapter 16

Erin, Vic, and Webb regrouped in the Major Crimes office. Rolf greeted his partner with a wag and a head cock, but he stayed sitting beside her desk until she released him. He wanted her to know he'd been standing good watch over the office.

"We got a confession, sir," Erin announced.

"Not that we needed it once we had that video," Vic added. "Good stuff."

"I suppose," Webb said. "We just need to put cameras everywhere and then we can all retire early."

"With everyone carrying Smartphones, we're practically there already," Erin said.

"It's creepy," Vic agreed. "Speaking of creeps, how'd you manage to keep from punching that video pervert right in the balls?"

"I'm a female cop," she reminded him. "When I was working Patrol, I dealt with creepy perverts practically every day. I couldn't punch them all."

"Me, too," Vic said. "Seriously, have you checked out this ass? Everybody wanted a piece." He turned to give her a profile view.

"None of us want to think about that, Neshenko," Webb said. He looked at the clock. "We're a couple hours past end of shift. I suppose you two want to be on your way..."

Erin and Vic looked hopefully at the door.

"...just as soon as you fill out your DD-5s," he finished.

"And there's the other shoe dropping," Erin said. "Bureaucratic paperwork."

"Don't blame the bureaucracy," Webb said. "You're the one who wanted to arrest everyone involved with this damned case."

"Yeah, are you going for some sort of departmental record?" Vic asked. He started counting on his fingers. "Let's see, we've got Stone for the actual murder, Polk and Schilling both on possession and resisting arrest, Feldspar for spying on hotel patrons, Caldwell for aiding and abetting... I'm just surprised you didn't bust the cleaning lady while you were at it."

"Shit," Erin said. "We were in such a hurry, we forgot."

"Josefina," Webb said, nodding.

"Who's Josefina?" Vic asked, utterly confused.

"One of the cleaning ladies," Erin explained. "She helped Caldwell move the body."

"So we *are* arresting someone else? What're we waiting for?" Vic started for the stairs.

"Go on," Webb said, waving a hand. "I'll get started on the paperwork, because I'm in a good mood. But don't think you're getting out of all of it. It'll be waiting for you when you get back."

"I guess it's good to have things to look forward to," Erin said as she, Vic, and Rolf jogged downstairs.

"Yeah," Vic said. "Like death."

"You look forward to death?"

"All Russians do. Just look at the world. Being dead's gotta be an improvement over this."

"Vic, is there more to Russian culture than alcohol and suicide?"

"Is there more to Irish culture than alcohol and getting the shit kicked out of you by the British?"

"We write some pretty good poetry."

"So do we." Vic paused. "Not that I read Russian poetry in my spare time."

"If I was interrogating you, I'd call that a suspiciously specific denial," Erin said.

They got into Erin's car, Rolf eagerly climbing in yet again, and set off once more for the InterContinental.

"Answer me this," Vic said after a couple of minutes. "Our girl gets killed in an upscale hotel. Not only isn't it a secret, but practically everybody knows about it. Am I right?"

"You're right," Erin said. "The manager knew, the security chief knew, all of them were just pretending to help us and hoping we'd think it was some sort of crazy accident. Which I guess it was, come to think of it. But yeah, even the cleaning staff knew."

"And we were pretty much the only ones who didn't," Vic went on.

"Right again," she said. "Is there a point you're getting to?"

"It just seems like a lot of wasted effort. I mean, anybody could've come to us, anytime, and told the truth. Why does everybody always lie to us?"

"Does it hurt your feelings, Vic?"

"A little, yeah."

"I didn't know you were so sensitive."

"I'm serious, Erin. We could've closed this one in five minutes if just one person had done the right thing."

"They'd all done things wrong," she said. "Telling on Stone would've implicated them. By your thinking, we could solve every murder if the murderer would just tell us the truth. I mean, they tend to know they killed someone."

"That's true," he said. Then he snapped his fingers. "Forget the cameras. What we need is truth serum."

"Sodium pentothal doesn't really work," she said. "It just makes people loose and talkative. It doesn't make them tell the truth."

"Too bad." He brooded on that for a moment. "On the bright side, I guess it's job security."

* * *

Josefina might be long gone by now. Erin felt like an idiot. They'd been too much of a rush and she'd forgotten that last loose end. Finding an illegal immigrant in New York who didn't want to be found was a needle-in-the-haystack kind of thing. But there was nothing to do but try to see it through.

They found a chaotic scene in the hotel lobby. CSU techs were going in and out of the manager's office, patrons were milling around and talking excitedly, the hotel staff were trying to keep order, and uniformed officers were scattered throughout the room, either trying to help or just watching and loitering.

Vic's massive bulk, coupled with his badly-swollen face, cleared a path to the front desk. The detectives found the assistant manager, a pale, skinny guy. He had on a pair of wire-rimmed glasses that kept slipping down his nose. The tag on his chest read Niemann.

"You in charge?" Vic asked.

"No," Niemann said. He made an angry gesture at the crowd, then had to bring his hand up to his face to save his glasses from flying off. "Nobody's in charge. Are you more cops?"

"Detectives," Erin said. They presented their gold shields.

"Then maybe you can get this circus on the road so we can get back to business," Niemann said. "You've arrested our manager. Everybody's trying to figure out why. They're being disorderly, which is a problem because you also arrested our head of security! Can either of you tell me what's going on?"

"CSU will be out of your hair as quickly as possible," Erin said. "I apologize for any inconvenience. We just need to take care of a few things. I understand you have a Josefina on your housekeeping staff?"

"Josefina?" Niemann pushed his glasses up his nose, where they immediately began sliding down again. "Yes. Josefina Molina. Head housekeeper. She's been here for... I don't know, longer than I have. Years. We've never had a problem with her. What could you possibly need her for?"

"If we could just speak with her, it'd be great," Erin said. "Is she on duty?"

"She just came on. She works nights most of the time."

"Where can we find her?" Erin asked.

"If she's not cleaning a room, she's probably up in the laundry."

"Where's that?" Vic asked.

"Fourth floor. But what are you going to do about this mess?"

"Talk to the ranking officer on scene," Erin suggested. "Thanks for your help."

"But which one...?" Niemann began helplessly.

Vic and Erin were already on their way to the elevators, Rolf keeping pace. Vic hit the call button and soon they were on their way up. Erin stood against the back wall of the elevator, a smile at one corner of her mouth.

"What's so funny?" Vic asked.

"It's a language thing," she said. "I know a little German, mostly on account of Rolf."

"So?"

"Our manager's name, Niemann. Know what it means?"

"I speak Russian, Erin. It's got a whole different alphabet than German. Russians don't speak German. Russians *shoot* Germans."

Rolf cocked his head and gave Vic a quizzical stare.

"It means 'nobody,'" Erin said. "We were talking to an actual, literal nobody."

"That's a lousy name to get stuck with," he said.

"What's Neshenko mean?" she asked.

"I got no idea. I mostly figure it means me. How about you?"

"O'Reilly? It just means 'from Reilly.'"

"I coulda guessed that. Where the hell is Reilly?"

"It's not a place. It's a clan."

"Oh. So there's a lot of you around, I guess."

"It's New York City, Vic. Of course there's a lot of Irish around. Yeah, there's a lot of O'Reillys. A bunch still in Ireland, too. My dad told me we don't get along with the O'Rourkes, but God only knows why."

"Probably something your great-great-great-whatever did to theirs, or maybe the other way round. People come to America to get away from that blood feud shit. So we gonna deport this Josefina? Send her back to whatever family shit the Molinas have going on in Mexico with the Rodriguezes or whoever?"

"I don't know yet."

He scowled. "I don't like playing ICE."

"Neither do I. But our girl aided in covering up a murder. She committed a crime, Vic. Look, let's just find out what she has to say. Then we'll figure out what to do."

The first thing Erin noticed on entering the laundry was the thrum of washing machines. The vibrations went through the floor and right up her legs, making her teeth want to chatter. Some sort of Latin pop music was playing over the sound of the machines, but they provided a constant bass accompaniment. The air was humid, with a visible haze of steam. Rolf sniffed the air and got a snout full of fabric softener. He snorted and shook his head.

Three Hispanic women were folding sheets and talking to each other in Spanish. They didn't notice the new arrivals at first. As Vic and Erin got closer, they saw two of the women were older, probably mid-forties, and the other was very young.

"Excuse me," Erin said.

All three women fell abruptly silent. They looked at Erin without much interest, but Vic seemed to alarm them. Maybe it was his size and broken-up face, but Erin had the feeling it was mostly that he was male. Something about the way they stared at him made her realize just how out-of-place he was.

"We're looking for Josefina Molina," Erin said.

The three women continued to stare without speaking. Maybe they didn't speak English. Maybe they were choosing not to understand English. Their faces were unreadable.

"Hey, Vic?" she said quietly. "Why don't you wait outside?"

He started to say something indignant. Then he saw the meaningful look she was giving him. He nodded, turned, and left the room.

The tension eased slightly. "You are lost, no?" one of the older women asked Erin in heavily-accented English. "You looking for bathroom?"

"Josefina Molina," Erin repeated.

The other older woman stepped forward, pushing gently but decisively past her two companions. Erin realized they'd been shielding her.

"What do you want?" Josefina asked. She was a stout, sturdy woman with a face and hands lined with a lifetime of work. Her skin was slightly wrinkled but as tough as boot leather. Her eyes were very dark, very sharp, and very intelligent.

"Ma'am, my name is Erin O'Reilly. I'm a detective with the New York Police Department. And I think you know why I'm here."

Josefina nodded slowly. "Yes. I will come with you. *Un momento, por favor.*"

Erin watched Josefina as the housekeeper turned and spoke to the two other laundresses. Erin was ready for trouble. Sometimes perps would act quiet right up to the last moment, then fight or run for it. Josefina didn't look like she meant to resist, but you could never tell.

The conversation was short, just a few sentences. Then Josefina turned back to face her. "I am ready." She put out her hands, wrists close together, ready for the handcuffs.

"That won't be necessary right now," Erin said. "We need to talk to you. Is there a place we can go, somewhere quiet?"

Josefina seemed startled, but nodded. "Yes, we have a room there." She pointed over her shoulder.

Erin cracked the laundry door. "Vic, c'mon," she said. He and Rolf followed the women through the laundry to the back, where a door opened onto a small break room. It had a card table and some folding chairs, an ancient television set, and an old couch that could have been the twin of the disreputable sofa in the Major Crimes break room.

"Whoa," Vic said. "I haven't seen rabbit ears on a TV in years. Does that thing still work?"

Josefina and Erin ignored him. The housekeeper pointed to one of the chairs for Erin and sat down opposite her.

"We caught him," Erin said. "The guy who killed the girl upstairs."

Josefina's face didn't change at all.

"And Caldwell, the security guy," she went on. "We know all about him. We've got him in custody. We know what happened." She paused. "All of it."

Josefina didn't blink.

"Ma'am," Erin said. "We know you took Sarah Devers out of Room 503. Why did you put her in the aquarium?"

"*Señor* Caldwell told me to clean up the mess," Josefina said. "He told me, clean up the room, take the *chica* away. He said if I did not do this, he would call Immigration. He told me to take the *chica* and put her somewhere no one would know what had happened to her."

"Did he tell you to put her in the fish tank?"

"No. I did that."

"Why?"

Josefina's eyes flashed. "It was not right, what happened to her. I am glad you caught them, these bad men. I thought, if I put her in one of the other rooms, maybe the wrong person would be punished. So I put her where I knew she would be found quickly. I hoped you would learn what had happened."

"But you could have just told us," Erin said.

"I could not have you know I was the one," Josefina said. "For my family, I did this. But if *Señor* Caldwell is in jail, then everything is all right. You do what you want with me. Send me back to Mexico, it is all right now."

"I don't understand," Erin said. "If you were worried about being deported, why are you okay with it now?"

"You do not understand, *señora*. He did not threaten to send me back. I will do all you ask, only do nothing to Rosa."

"Rosa?" Vic exclaimed. "Rosa Hernandez? The maid? What's she got to do with any of this?"

"I wanted to come to this country many years ago," Josefina said. "My husband was already across the border, working here. But he could not get permission to bring me. I was going to have a baby soon. I knew if I had the baby in America, then my child would be American and could not be deported. But on the way, before I could cross over, it was my time. I had my baby in a dry river. I was bleeding. I thought I would die. There was a man with us, a kind man. I begged him to take my child to my husband, so she would not die with me. He took her. His name was Jose Hernandez."

"Hernandez," Erin repeated.

"A *ranchero* found me that night. He took me to hospital in Mexico. I was sick for a long time. When I got better, I wrote to my husband, telling him what had happened."

Josefina looked down at her hands. "He never answered."

"Did you find out what happened to him?" Erin asked.

She nodded. "He was struck by a car. A driver who had been drinking. He never saw his daughter, never knew he had a child."

"So how did you end up here?" Vic asked.

"It was another year before I could save the money to pay a coyote to take me across the border," Josefina said, using the slang term for someone who smuggled immigrants. "He took me to El Paso. From there, I tried to find my daughter."

She laughed quietly, bitterly. "Jose Hernandez is a common name. A very common name. But I asked and asked, and I found someone who remembered a man with a newborn baby. I followed him. Six months, I followed, all the way to New York City. And there I found him. And I found my Rosa."

"What did you do when you found her?" Erin asked, thinking this woman would have made a good detective.

"She was almost two years old," Josefina said. "I had no papers, no family, no life. Jose had a wife and two other children. Rosa was happy, she thought he was her papa. I spoke with Jose, I told him I would be no trouble, I would take her if he did not want her, but I would not fight him.

"Jose is a good man. He loves my Rosa as his own. She thinks of him as her papa. I am a friend, nothing more. I watched my Rosa grow up an American girl, but she has no birth certificate. She was born in Mexico, on the wrong side of the border.

"I do not know how *Señor* Caldwell learned of her situation."

"No secrets in this damn place," Vic muttered. "Somebody always sees."

Josefina nodded. "He told me he would make sure Rosa was taken away from the only life she has known, from everyone who loved her. I could not let this happen, so I said I would do what he asked. But I am glad you have caught him. If you had not," her eyes flashed again, "I would have made sure he could not hurt my Rosa."

Erin held up a hand. "Don't say anything about that," she warned. "So you went along with Caldwell under coercion? He threatened your child?"

Josefina nodded.

"And Rosa doesn't know anything about this?"

"No. I wish she had not seen the *chica* in the water. I am sorry."

"You understand we can't charge him with what he threatened to do," Erin said. "Not without bringing Miss Hernandez into this and endangering her status."

"I understand."

"Erin," Vic said in an undertone. "We can't throw this lady out of the country over this. I'm not gonna do it."

"Neither am I," she replied. "And I don't think ICE has to hear anything about it. All we need to hear is that Ms. Molina was threatened by Caldwell and deliberately left the body where we'd find it. She's cooperating with our investigation. I'll recommend we not file any charges against her."

Josefina seemed stunned. "You are not sending me back to Mexico?"

"Ma'am," Erin said. "You went through more for your kid than anybody I know. You're maybe the only person in this mess who tried to do the right thing. I'm not going to be the one to punish you for it."

"Me, neither," Vic added.

"*Gracias, señora,*" Josefina said.

"You'll need to come down to the station and make an official statement," Erin said. "I'm sorry for the inconvenience."

"You may want to think a little about what you're gonna say," Vic added. "There's some stuff in there you might wanna leave out."

"What my partner is saying," Erin said, "is that you only need to put what's relevant to the murder in your statement. No point adding a lot of other stuff that'll only take up space and confuse people. Do you understand?"

"I understand," Josefina said. "And I understand you are a good woman. And you are a good man," she added, turning to Vic.

"I wouldn't go quite that far," Vic said.

"I will pray for both of you," she said.

"Thanks," Erin said. "We can use it."

Chapter 17

By the time Erin finally left the Eightball, she felt like she'd worked two straight shifts back to back. Mathematically, that was true. She and Vic had turned up at the station around nine that morning. Now, after Josefina's statement and all the arrest reports, incident reports, and associated paperwork, they'd been on the clock better than fifteen hours. She needed a drink, and then she needed to go home and get some sleep. Fortunately, those goals were now more compatible than ever.

Bleary-eyed and stiff, she loaded Rolf into the Charger and drove to the Barley Corner. She pulled into the parking garage two storefronts down from the pub. The parking attendant nodded politely to her when she pulled in. She recognized one of Carlyle's guys. Of course they ran the parking garage. A man who'd built car bombs for the IRA wasn't about to leave his ride in the care of some random minimum-wage teenager. She parked in one of the spots reserved for the Corner, next to an empty space where Carlyle's gray Mercedes usually sat. He could be almost anywhere. Mob guys did most of their business after sundown. The annoying thing was, he ought to be home recuperating.

Erin gave Rolf a quick turn around the block so he could piss on a couple of lampposts. Then she walked into the bar. There was no secrecy to it, no reason to hide. Half the New York underworld probably knew by now that she'd taken up residence.

"Hey, Erin! How's it going?"

"How's the bad-ass bitch?"

"It's the finest of New York's finest! C'mon in!"

The calls that met her were raucous and a little offensive, but friendly. Erin realized, as she walked across the room, that these guys, blue-collar criminals, compulsive gamblers, drunks, and thugs, had adopted her as one of their own. She'd gotten in because she was Carlyle's girl, but something in the way they spoke to her now suggested she was standing on her own merits.

As she approached the bar, a big, burly guy with hairy arms and a bushy beard stood up, making room for her. He clapped her on the shoulder with a grin.

"I know you?" she asked.

"Robbie Exley," he said, seeming pleased she'd asked. "The boys call me Express. Can I buy you a drink?"

"Thanks, Express," she said, returning the smile. "But I don't pay for drinks here."

"Hell, I know that," he said. "Everybody knows that. I just wanna say thanks."

"What for?" Erin was suddenly wary, but Exley's face was friendly, in spite of a nasty scar on his left cheek, and his hands were open and empty.

"Wayne's a good buddy. I hear you kept the Staties from screwing him."

Then she understood. The nickname, the connection with Wayne, his presence in this bar all came together. Exley was a

Teamster, another of Corky's guys and probably a smuggler. Word had gotten around.

"Forget about it," she said. "Just making sure everybody got where they needed to go."

"You're all right," Exley said. "You ever need something, just ask for Express."

He shambled off to join some other guys by the dart board. Erin watched him go and smiled quizzically. The enhancement to her underworld reputation felt good, but she knew it shouldn't. She'd have to get used to those conflicting feelings, just like she'd have to get used to being a minor celebrity with these guys.

"Evening, Erin!" the bartender said. "What can I get you?"

"Usual, Danny."

"Single or double?"

"I'm at the end of a double shift. What do you think?"

"Coming right up," he said with a smile. He pulled down a bottle of Glen D whiskey and a glass. He poured a stiff double shot and slid it across the bar.

Erin picked up the glass and raised it to her lips.

Then she saw the woman at the far end of the bar. Erin choked on the whiskey. The liquor shot up the back of her nasal passage, leaving trails of liquid fire. She bent over the bar, coughing.

Danny was instantly there. "Hey, you all right?" he asked, putting a hand on her upper back.

Erin nodded and wiped at her streaming eyes. "Yeah," she croaked.

"You sure?"

"Just had a little go down the wrong way." Once her eyes had cleared, she looked again, making sure she hadn't imagined what she'd seen.

A tall, dark-haired woman with striking good looks was sitting at the bar, sipping a cocktail. A familiar tall, dark-haired woman. A couple of patrons were talking her up, obviously flirting. She was smiling and laughing at something one of them had said.

Erin set her half-empty glass on the bar and stalked toward the woman. Rolf paced beside her. He'd picked up on the sudden change in her energy. His hackles were rising and his walk was tense and stiff-legged. He smelled trouble.

The man on the woman's left said something else, some joke or other, and put a hand on the back of her wrist. The woman, still laughing, playfully swatted at the hand but didn't really try to shoo him off.

Erin came up on the man's blind side. "Take a hike, buddy," she said in a low, hard voice.

"What's it to you?" he shot back, hardly turning away from his target.

"She's my sister-in-law," Erin growled. "Get your hand off her before I break it."

"Erin?" Michelle O'Reilly said, surprised but still smiling. "Hi! Have a seat!"

Erin looked down at Michelle's arm. The guy was still resting his hand there. She reached across and grabbed the back of his hand. She pulled and twisted it sharply clockwise, stepping back from the bar as she did.

It was a simple, basic move that didn't require much strength. Leverage and momentum did most of the work. The man, a big strong-looking guy, went off his bar stool with a squawk of surprise. He managed to catch himself on his knees, his arm splayed uncomfortably out in front of him.

Erin put a little more pressure on the hand, bending it back toward his wrist.

"I said, get your hand off her," she said.

A space suddenly cleared around them, patrons hurriedly backing away. Dead silence fell, broken only by the television.

The man's friend was coming around behind Michelle, apparently intending to offer some assistance. He stopped short when he saw who was holding the guy. Or maybe it was the ninety-pound K-9 at her side, hair bristling, a low growl rising in the dog's chest.

"Beat it, numbnuts," said a gravelly voice behind Erin. It sounded like Express. Erin risked a quick glance over her shoulder and saw half a dozen guys backing her up. The trucker was holding a beer bottle by the neck in an ambiguously threatening grip.

"This isn't your problem," she said. "We've got no problem at all, isn't that right?"

The man whose arm she was holding nodded, suddenly very eager to please. "No problem."

"You were apologizing to the lady," Erin prompted.

"Sorry, ma'am," he babbled. "I didn't mean no disrespect."

"And you were leaving," she went on, adding a little more pressure.

He nodded more frantically. Erin let go and pushed. He flailed and almost fell over. Then he scrambled to his feet and fled the bar, his comrade right on his heels.

Exley shrugged and gave Erin a smile. "Hey," he said. "It didn't look like a private fight. I didn't mean to step on your toes. You had it covered."

"Erin! What are you doing?" Michelle exclaimed. Her face was a combination of stunned surprise and outrage.

"What the hell are you doing here, Shelley?" Erin hissed, leaning in close and speaking in a fierce whisper. "This is a dangerous place!"

"Your mom was here," Michelle protested. "How bad could it be?"

"You don't know these guys!"

"You live here!"

"Yeah, and you don't! Does Junior know where you are?"

Anger was rapidly eclipsing surprise in Michelle's face. "I don't ask him where he is all the time," she snapped. "And it's frankly none of your business."

"He's my brother!"

"And he's my husband!"

"I'm guessing he's working a night shift?" Erin said. "While you're here at a bar, flirting with strangers?"

"I came here to see you! The bartender said he thought you'd be in sometime this evening. I was just talking."

"How long have you been sitting here?" Erin demanded. "What about your kids?"

"The kids are fine. Your mom's staying over."

"Does she know where you are?" Erin was appalled.

"No, she's asleep, of course. It's after midnight. Look, Erin, nothing happened. No harm done."

"I could've broken that jerk's arm," Erin said.

"I didn't ask you to do anything! What's the matter with you, Erin? I wanted to come see you, see your place, how you're living now. I thought maybe I'd finally meet this guy you've moved in with."

"Where is he, anyway?" Erin wondered aloud.

She looked at Danny. The bartender had drifted to this end of the bar when the altercation had started. Now he was standing there, trying not to look like he was hovering.

"Hey, Danny, where's Carlyle?"

"At a meeting with Evan, I think," Danny said. "Corky's there, too."

"He going to be back soon?"

Danny shrugged. "Got me. Everything okay here? No trouble?"

"Nothing I couldn't handle."

The bartender nodded and moved off to handle other customers. Erin and Michelle were left to their own devices. Rolf, still bristling, sat next to Erin and watched the room.

"Seriously, Shelley," Erin said. "What were you thinking? You're a good-looking woman. You come into a place like this, late at night, by yourself, you're going to get hit on."

"Maybe that's what I wanted," Michelle said sulkily. "Maybe I just wanted to get out of the house and feel like a woman for a change, instead of a housewife. You don't know what it's like, Erin."

"No, I don't," Erin said grimly.

"Look, if you're ashamed of this place, or of what you do, you just have to tell me," Michelle said.

"It's not that," Erin said. "It's just... I don't know how to explain it. You're right, I'm not your chaperone. I just don't want you to get into trouble."

Then Michelle smiled suddenly, the anger draining out of her. "From what I could see, half the men in this place were ready to fight for you," she said. "I think I'm as safe here as anywhere in New York."

Thinking of safety made Erin wonder where Ian was. Surely he would have intervened in a fight. But then she remembered the missing Mercedes. Ian was Carlyle's driver. They'd be together, wherever they were.

"Okay," she said. "But remember, people are always watching. There's some rough guys hanging around this place."

"Ooh, adventurous," Michelle said.

"I mean it, Shelley. Just don't go down any back alleys with anyone."

Michelle nodded. "Okay, okay, message received. Now, are you going to show me your new apartment or what?"

"Can we do this some other time? I've been working all day and I'm tired." Erin didn't have it in her to play hostess, not after everything that had happened.

"Fine." Michelle pouted a little. "But don't think you can hide this guy from me forever. Now that your mom's met him, you've got no excuse."

"I'll introduce you," Erin said. "We'll set something up. Now I need to go to bed, and you probably want some sleep, too."

"Fine," Michelle said again. "You're a little overprotective, has anyone ever told you that?"

"I'm a cop. What do you expect?"

Michelle gave Erin a quick hug and kiss on the cheek. Then she patted Rolf on the head, left a couple of bills on the bar, and made for the door. Erin watched her go.

Her heart froze for a second. There, standing next to the door, was Mickey Connor. The enforcer, arms crossed, was watching Michelle. Then he looked away from the other woman and met Erin's stare.

Erin made herself look right back into Mickey's flat, pale blue eyes, as empty as a vacant lot. How long had he been there? What had he seen? What did he know? In this world, everyone was always watching, looking for weak spots or advantages.

Erin took a deep breath. This was the world she'd chosen to live in. Still holding Mickey's eye, she walked back to her previous place at the bar, picked up her glass, and finished her drink. The whiskey burned its way down into her belly.

"Go on and look, you son of a bitch," she muttered through clenched teeth. "We'll see who blinks first."

*   *   *

"I hear you had a bit of excitement downstairs," Carlyle said.

Erin tried not to jump up from the couch in the living room she was still trying to think of as hers. But it was hard. She'd told herself he met with Evan O'Malley all the time, that there was nothing to worry about, but Evan had people killed, damn it. And here it was, long after midnight. She should have been asleep hours ago, but how was she supposed to do that when her boyfriend was talking to a murderous sociopath?

She stood up and met him at the top of the stairs, giving him a smile and a kiss. "Nothing much," she said. "Just a little misunderstanding. I handled it."

"So I understand," he said, returning the smile. "Danny told me."

"What about you and Corky? Everything go all right? Does Evan suspect anything?"

"Darling, you have to stop thinking like that," he said, taking her hands. "If you start jumping at shadows, you'll be seeing them everywhere. Unless we know something concrete, we've no choice but to assume Evan doesn't know."

She made a face. "If he finds out, the first concrete thing could be a pair of cement shoes."

"We don't really do that, darling."

"I know. It's a figure of speech."

"Of course he's watching, and of course he's suspicious," Carlyle said. "A mathematician, a German lad called Schrödinger, said a cat could be both alive and dead at the same time. The act of observing the cat decided its fate. That's how it goes in the Life, too. If they see the wrong thing, you die. You mustn't let it affect you. Just remember, while they're watching you, you're watching them right back. Let them be nervous. It's all part of the game."

"Some game," she said. "If you lose, you die."

"Aye, that's the way of it," he said. "But with you, at least, I've a chance to win. That's something."

Keep reading for a sneak peek from

The Devil You Know
The Erin O'Reilly Mysteries, Book 13

Here's a sneak peek from Book 13: The Devil You Know

Coming 9/27/21

Erin O'Reilly stared at the painting on the museum wall. She didn't know much about art, though she'd once held a painting worth millions of dollars. The painting in front of her wasn't for sale, had never been appraised. But it hung here in the Guggenheim, in the heart of Manhattan, in a place of honor, so it had to be worth something.

The artist hadn't used the traditional oil on canvas of so many masters. This painter had opted for watercolors on some sort of heavy paper. A commentary on the impermanence of everything, even art? She'd heard Tibetan monks liked to make art out of colored sand, which blew away in the next strong wind.

Erin peered closer, trying to decipher the image. She saw eyes, big blue ones with cartoonishly enlarged curled lashes, atop a toothy grin so white it suggested very good dental care. The background was yellow, which she thought of as a happy color.

"Auntie Erin?"

Erin became aware of a tugging on the leg of her slacks. She looked down to see her niece, one hand curled into the fabric of her slacks, the other poking meditatively into the corner of her mouth.

"What's up, kiddo?" she asked.

"I'm bored."

Erin dropped to one knee so they were eye to eye. "Why's that?" she asked.

"We're in a museum," Anna said.

"So?"

"Museums are bo-ring." The nine-year-old stretched the word out as far as it would go.

"Look at this stuff," Erin said. "These things were all made by kids, some of them your own age. Now they're hanging here for grown-ups to look at, just like any artist. Isn't that neat?"

"I guess, but I've seen them. Now I'm bored."

Erin smiled. She supposed the Guggenheim's annual Year with Children exhibit was something a girl Anna's age might soon tire of. She ruffled the kid's hair affectionately.

"Look, you still want to be a cop when you grow up?"

"I'm going to be a detective just like you," Anna said in tones of absolute certainty.

"You know, detectives spend a lot of time on stakeouts. Do you know what that is?"

"Yeah. When you sit in your car waiting to catch the bad guys."

"Exactly. And do you know what we do while we wait for them?"

Anna thought about it. She shook her head.

"We just sit, usually in the dark," Erin said. "For hours. You have to learn to be patient."

Anna considered this. "What do you do when you have to go potty?" she asked with a pre-teen's practicality.

"We hold it. Or we use an empty paper cup."

"Really? Eww!" Anna wrinkled her nose. "But you can't get out of your car for anything?"

"If we did, the bad guys might see us," Erin explained. "So we just have to wait. Like you and I have to wait for your mom and brother."

"But you get food while you wait, right?" Anna asked.

"Yeah, we eat in the car."

"I want ice cream," Anna declared.

"I haven't got it in my pockets, kiddo," Erin said.

"Ice cream," Anna said again, crossing her arms. "If we're on stakeout, I want ice cream."

"You're going to end up a union rep for sure," Erin said. "They'll like a negotiator like you. Tell you what. We'll go looking for your mom and Patrick. When we find them, I'll ask about the ice cream. If your mom says it's okay, then we can have it."

"Yaaay!" Anna said. She grabbed Erin's hand and tugged enthusiastically.

They found Michelle O'Reilly and Patrick in the next room, in front of a display of clay sculptures that looked like fluorescent-colored dinosaurs of some sort. Patrick was trying to reach past his mother to get his hands on one of them.

Michelle was trying to steer him clear of the display. So far it seemed to be a draw.

"I've got a vote for ice cream," Erin announced.

"Oh, thank God," Michelle said. "Sean wanted another kid. I should've talked him into a pet squirrel instead. It'd be less work. Let's go." Patrick, seeing her momentary distraction, tried to slip past her. Michelle, without even looking, snared him with a deft forearm and scooped him up into her arms. He wriggled, trying to escape, and she tickled him. He was soon reduced to helpless squeals.

"Motherhood, huh?" Erin said as Anna pulled her toward the exit and Michelle followed, still carrying the youngest O'Reilly.

"It's the greatest gift a woman can have," Michelle said. "Or so everyone keeps telling me." But she was smiling. Michelle was a tall, strikingly attractive woman a few years older than Erin. She'd married Erin's brother, a trauma surgeon at Bellevue Hospital, and bucked the conventional wisdom of the twenty-first century by deciding to be a housewife and mother. Today she'd spent the morning with her kids and her sister-in-law the Major Crimes detective.

"Anna got bored," Erin explained in an undertone.

"Are you kidding? This is the most excitement I've had all week," Michelle said.

"Excitement isn't all it's cracked up to be," Erin said. "Just be glad you're not tripping over dead bodies all day."

"It does put my life in a little perspective," Michelle said. "My husband spends his time saving lives, his sister catches killers, and I go to PTA meetings."

"You've got a couple of great kids," Erin said.

"I know," Michelle said, still smiling. "I guess the grass is always greener."

It was a good couple of blocks to the nearest supermarket, on Madison Avenue, but it was a pleasant, sunny day and Anna's energy carried them along. Erin was enjoying her day off, though she missed her partner. Her K-9, Rolf, was back at Michelle and Sean Junior's Midtown brownstone, hopefully having a nice nap.

"How's your boyfriend?" Michelle asked.

"He's doing well," Erin said. "He can get around a lot better now. They say he's going to make a full recovery."

It was still a little strange to be openly talking to her family about her boyfriend. She and Morton Carlyle had kept their relationship secret right until a would-be assassin had shot him in the stomach right in the middle of Erin's living room. After that, things had gotten complicated. Carlyle was a gangster, Erin was a cop, and the two of them were trying their best to thread their way through the obstacle course their love life had become. Carlyle was ostensibly working for the NYPD now as an informant, but it would be a while before they accumulated enough evidence to move on his associates in the O'Malley mob. In the meantime, Erin figured she'd take a quiet, sunny day with the family. It beat getting shot at.

"I still need to meet him," Michelle said.

"Soon," Erin promised.

"I hate that word," Anna said.

"Why?" Erin asked.

"When grown-ups use it, it means the same thing as 'never,'" Anna said.

"Smart kid," Erin remarked to Michelle.

*　　*　　*

Armed with Magnum ice cream bars, they emerged from the supermarket a quarter of an hour later. They started in the direction of Central Park. The plan was to get hot dogs from a cart somewhere along the way and have a picnic lunch.

"Life is uncertain," Michelle said. "Sometimes you should eat dessert first."

"Mommy?" Anna said in muffled tones.

"Don't talk with your mouth full, dear," Michelle said automatically.

"Mommy, that lady looks sick," Anna said, pointing.

"Don't stare and don't point," Michelle said. "It's rude."

Erin, as a police officer, had different standards of etiquette than civilians. Anything out of the ordinary was worth her attention, and she didn't care if someone thought she was staring. She followed Anna's gesture.

A blonde woman was weaving her way along the sidewalk. Her high-heeled, knee-high boots weren't made for stability and she kept stumbling. Her face was a ghastly smear of day-old makeup, scarlet lipstick painting a gash across her pale features. Her hair was a tangled mess of curls. Her eyes were hollow and staring, with pupils that belonged on another planet.

"She's not sick," Erin said quietly.

"Is she on drugs?" Anna asked loudly.

Michelle winced. But even though the blonde was less than twenty feet away, the other woman gave no sign that she'd heard.

"It's not even noon," Michelle muttered out of the side of her mouth. "You'd think she'd have the decency not to get hammered this early."

Erin had seen drunk or strung-out people at every hour of the day or night. Chemical dependency didn't operate on a nine-to-five schedule. But this woman looked harmless enough. The blonde was dressed for a wild night. Her long legs were clad in fishnet stockings that ran up under a very short miniskirt. Her halter-top was only barely decent. Even though it was a warm day, the woman was underdressed.

The blonde teetered past the O'Reillys. Then, abruptly, she swerved off the curb and stumbled into the street.

Erin's police instincts kicked in even before the first blare of a car horn. She sprinted toward the woman without taking time to think. Her half-eaten ice cream bar fell from her hand, forgotten, and splattered on the concrete. A white panel truck laid rubber on Fifth Avenue, fishtailing and trying to swerve out of the way.

Erin grabbed the woman's arm and yanked as hard as she could. The blonde, off-balance, tumbled toward her. They fell back together onto the curb. Erin felt a sharp pain in her side where the concrete dug into her. The truck continued on its way with a last irritable blast of its horn.

"What the hell were you thinking?" Erin snapped.

"Sorry," the blonde mumbled. "Couldn't... tell... where'm I?"

"New York," Erin said grimly, getting to her feet. She saw her family coming toward her and waved them back. "You could've been killed."

"Sorry," the woman said again, and Erin saw she was scarcely more than a girl under the caked-on makeup.

"What's your name?" Erin asked.

"Tammy." The girl sat on the curb and hugged her elbows.

"What are you doing out here, Tammy?"

"Looking..."

"Looking for what?"

Tammy squinted at Erin, trying to focus. "Help," she said, shaping her lips carefully and distinctly around the word.

"You need help?" Erin asked. "It's okay. I'm a detective. What do you need help with?"

"Not for me," Tammy said. "For him."

"Who?"

"Man... in the car."

"What man? What car?"

"Nice car. Fancy."

"Did a man in a nice car do something to you?" Erin asked. This was looking like a potential sexual assault case.

"Don't... remember."

"Where is the man?"

"In the car."

"Where's the car?"

Tammy waved her hand vaguely back the direction she'd come from.

"Were you in the car?" Erin asked.

Tammy nodded.

"Do you know this man?" Erin pressed.

"Don't know. Don't think so. Head... hurts." Tammy pressed a hand against her forehead.

"Why does he need help?"

"I think... think he's... dead."

Ready for more?

Join Steven Henry's author email list
for the latest on new releases, upcoming books and
series, behind-the-scenes details, events, and more.

Be the first to know about the release of Book 2 in
the Erin O'Reilly Mysteries by signing up at
tinyurl.com/StevenHenryEmail

About the Author

Steven Henry learned how to read almost before he learned how to walk. Ever since he began reading stories, he wanted to put his own on the page. He lives a very quiet and ordinary life in Minnesota with his wife and dog.

Also by Steven Henry

Ember of Dreams
The Clarion Chronicles, Book One

When magic awakens a long-forgotten folk, a noble lady, a young apprentice, and a solitary blacksmith band together to prevent war and seek understanding between humans and elves.

Lady Kristyn Tremayne – An otherwise unremarkable young lady's open heart and inquisitive mind reveal a hidden world of magic.

Robert Blackford – A humble harp maker's apprentice dreams of being a hero.

Master Gabriel Zane – A master blacksmith's pursuit of perfection leads him to craft an enchanted sword, drawing him out of his isolation and far from his cozy home.

Lord Luthor Carnarvon – A lonely nobleman with a dark past has won the heart of Kristyn's mother, but at what cost?

Readers love *Ember of Dreams*

"The more I got to know the characters, the more I liked them. The female lead in particular is a treat to accompany on her journey from ordinary to extraordinary."

"The author's deep understanding of his protagonists' motivations and keen eye for psychological detail make Robert and his companions a likable and memorable cast."

Learn more at tinyurl.com/emberofdreams.

More great titles from Clickworks Press

www.clickworkspress.com

Hubris Towers: The Complete First Season
Ben Y. Faroe & Bill Hoard

Comedy of manners meets comedy of errors in a new series for fans of Fawlty Towers and P. G. Wodehouse.

"So funny and endearing"

"Had me laughing so hard that I had to put it down to catch my breath"

"Astoundingly, outrageously funny!"

Learn more at clickworkspress.com/hts01.

The Dream World Collective
Ben Y. Faroe

Five friends quit their jobs to chase what they love. Rent looms. Hilarity ensues.

"If you like interesting personalities, hidden depths... and hilarious dialog, this is the book for you."

"a fun, inspiring read—perfect for a sunny summer day."

"a heartwarming, feel-good story"

Learn more at clickworkspress.com/dwc.

Death's Dream Kingdom
Gabriel Blanchard

A young woman of Victorian London has been transformed into a vampire. Can she survive the world of the immortal dead— or perhaps, escape it?

"The wit and humor are as Victorian as the setting... a winsomely vulnerable and tremendously crafted work of art."

"A dramatic, engaging novel which explores themes of death, love, damnation, and redemption."

Learn more at clickworkspress.com/ddk.

Share the love!

Join our microlending team at
kiva.org/team/clickworkspress.

Keep in touch!

Join the Clickworks Press email list
and get freebies, production updates, special deals,
behind-the-scenes sneak peeks, and more.

Sign up today at clickworkspress.com/join.

CPSIA information can be obtained
at www.ICGtesting.com
Printed in the USA
LVHW092057170721
692931LV00006B/796

9 781943 383771